The Game

J M Steele

Copyright © 2013 Juliana M. Steele

Published and distributed by Juliana M. Steele

Editing by First Editing

Cover Art by Bruce Rolff (www.shutterstock.com)

All rights reserved. No part of this book may be reproduced by any mechanical, photographic, digital, audio or electronic process; nor may be stored in a retrieval system, transmitted, or otherwise copied for public or private use – other than for "fair use" as brief quotations embodied in articles and reviews – without prior written permission of the author.

This is a work of fiction. Names, characters, places, and incidents are the product of the author's imagination and are used fictitiously. Any resemblance to actual events or locales, or persons living or deceased, is strictly coincidental.

Steele, Juliana M.

The Game / Juliana M. Steele. – 1st ed.

ISBN: Print on Demand - 978-0-9859513-0-6
eBook – 978-0-9859513-1-3

DEDICATION

This book is for anyone who thinks they can't..
YES, YOU CAN.

ACKNOWLEDGMENTS

This book would not be possible without the love and support of family and friends. I would like to thank my brother, Dan Steele, for his encouragement and honesty, and my husband, Ken Johnson, for his unwavering support and patience with my early morning and odd hour writing habits. I would also like to thank Peter at FirstEditing.com for his comments and suggestions - I could not have gotten through to the end without you – and Shutterstock.com for the cover art.

Table of CONTENTS

CHAPTER 1
CHAPTER 2
CHAPTER 3
CHAPTER 4
CHAPTER 5
CHAPTER 6
CHAPTER 7
CHAPTER 8
CHAPTER 9
CHAPTER 10
CHAPTER 11
CHAPTER 12
CHAPTER 13
CHAPTER 14
CHAPTER 15
CHAPTER 16
CHAPTER 17
CHAPTER 18
CHAPTER 19
ABOUT THE AUTHOR

CHAPTER 1

Jason laughed, as was usually the case when he felt like crying. "It's okay, Dad. I understand. These things happen." Yup, he thought. Shit happens. It just happens to you more than other people, I guess.

"That's my boy. I knew you'd understand. This account will mean big things for Elec-celence... and for me... and for us!"

I know, I know, thought Jason. He could hear his father's words, like a broken record, playing over and over in his head.

"Why, if I land this account, they can't refuse me that VP position. This could be the maker or breaker for me, Kiddo." Jason's father always called him "Kiddo" when he felt he had brought Jason to his side. "And you helped make it happen. I mean, you just say the word, Kiddo, and I'm on the next plane home. We'll be fishing by dawn tomorrow morning. But not you. You understand the big picture. Not like your mother. She never could get it... that this was all for her, and for you... and of course for Deenie too..."

"Sound good, Kiddo?" "Kiddo?" "Jason, are you there...?"

"Oh, yeah, sure, next time. Sounds good."

"Great! Gotta go. Give my love to Deenie and I'll see you in a few weeks." Click.

Yeah. See ya. I gotta go too. Have a nice sale, he thought. Kiddo.

"Jason. Are you okay?" His mom leaned against the door jam, her form silhouetted against the light of the kitchen beyond.

"Sure. Blow off Number One-million-nine-hundred-and-sixty-three. Piece of cake."

She smiled softly and stepped forward to tousle his hair. She was the only one who could still get away with that and she knew it. Jason looked at her, deeply, silently, and she enfolded him into her arms. Not a word; not a thought. He breathed in her motherliness and sighed.

Jason's mother, Liz, knew, and would always know, that place in Jason that hurt; that place that his father's arrows always hit. Damn him, she thought; and she sighed... once a bastard, always a bastard. And although she could not stop the pain, she could certainly be there for it, and for him. And for herself.

"Mom!... Mom! ...Mom-mie!"

"Coming, Deenie!" she called, as she unfolded herself from Jason's arms. Jason mused after her. How did she do it? With two kids and a part time job, she had the patience of a saint.

Jason followed the noise into the yard and came upon his sister, Deenie, trying—unsuccessfully—to give their cat, Spike, a bath. His mother had joined the fray and was - unsuccessfully as well - trying to rinse green goo from the disgruntled cat's hair. Jason fell back against the porch railing, arms across his stomach, and laughed so hard he cried. Spike was twisting first one way then the other, not sure whether to focus on avoiding the smaller annoyance or now the larger. The larger had water, though, so the poor cat focused its attention on avoiding the rinsing. His mother looked up with a mock frown. "Don't just lie there, come and help!" Jason sank to the steps, sprawled like a drunk, and continued to laugh, tears streaming down his cheeks. His mother, attempting to rinse a green-colored gel from good naturedly turned the hose on her only son and said, "Gosh, this thing is hard to control."

Jason, still chuckling, twisted out of the way of the spray and glided to his feet. He had his mother's finesse, and she looked on admiringly as she watched him escape in one fluid motion. She would have been hard-pressed for an answer if someone had asked her at that time which was more fluid, her son or the water. In the end, she would probably have opted for her son.

Jason strode towards the threesome and took the cat by the scruff of its neck. He glanced sidelong at his sister and asked, "What is this stuff anyway?"

"It's aloe," declared Deenie. She firmly planted her hands on her hips. "It's good for your skin. It keeps it from getting dry." Barely four, she had the wisdom of a sage, or at least she thought she did.

Jason frowned a bit. "I see, said the blind man," and he turned and winked at his mother. "Well, now that Spike has had an aloe bath and will have nice, soft, moist skin, he's all set, right?"

Deenie frowned. She had not thought that far yet.

"All rinsed," said Jason, and he let the cat go. Spike glared at Jason and sauntered off, finally coming to rest on the picnic table, so he could handle his own grooming in peace.

Jason watched him a moment and then turned his attention to Deenie. "Deenie's turn!" he cried, and as he started toward her, she ran into the house, trailing screams.

Jason laughed as his mother tried to muster a frown.

"You shouldn't tease your sister like that," she said.

"Yeah, right, next time," he replied, sporting a cat-like grin. His mother shook her head, stepped forward, and tousled his hair for the second time that day.

After dinner, Deenie helped clear the table as Jason began to do the dishes. Ever since his dad had left three years ago, it just seemed right to him that they should all help. He remembered back to the days when his dad was still there. His dad had virtually forbid him, or anyone, from helping in the kitchen.

"Your mom's got one job and one job only, and that's to take care of me and you kids," he would say. "Now, if you go around taking care of yourself, kiddo, what's your mom gonna have to do?"

Although there was logic there, in a strange sense of the word, Jason never felt very good with that philosophy, not even at twelve. Now, at the ripe old age of fifteen he was even more sure that he didn't like it, and now that he really thought about it, there were a lot more of his dad's philosophies that he didn't really like.

"Mom," said Jason, pausing from the dishes to look at her, "if dad has so much money, how come you worked when you were married to him?"

Liz smiled. "So, my little man is becoming inquisitive in his old age." Jason returned the smile with a grin that melted her heart. *No matter what pain and suffering that bastard throws our way, Jason always seems to muddle through,* she thought with a sigh.

"I worked because I wanted to," she said. "I had a job before I met your dad, in a design firm. The owner, Claudia, she taught me everything she knew. When I met and married our dad, even though he had a good job and enough money so that I would never have to work, I wanted to keep working. I enjoyed working, it gave me a sense of self-satisfaction ... a certain pride in myself," And, as she stretched her head high and puffed out her chest, she continued, with a gleam in her eye," a pride that being Mrs. Andrew Coussens could not."

Jason watched her. His mom was beautiful, even at 37. Not a line crossed her face, and her glossy blonde hair piled on her head in a make-shift bun. Coupled with her blue eyes and pouty, fleshy lips, she was attractive by any standards, even if you were fifteen.

Jason turned back to his dishes, and his mother sighed again, staring into space.

"Your father and I had some good years, Jason, and we had some bad." She turned to him, suddenly serious. "And from that marriage came you. And Deenie. For those reasons alone it was all worthwhile."

Jason stared hard at the sink. Sudsy water… a few stray knives and forks. Interesting how when the soap starts to de-sud, the last few bubbles cling to the sides of the sink. As if by holding onto something they could stop the dissolving process. His mother and he were close - closer than mothers and sons ought to be – his father was fond of telling him. But their conversations didn't ever seem to get this deep. Theirs was more of a telepathic relationship. She felt his pain and he felt hers, and they comforted one another in silence, without ever having to open their wounds for the other to see. He wasn't quite sure he liked this new arrangement.

"Deenie needs tucking in," she said, and headed toward the stairs.

"Mom..." Jason started, as he spun around to catch a glimpse of her as she started up the stairs. She turned her head toward him, smiled, and resumed her climb. Jason continued to stare at the stairs, knowing somehow things were changing, and yet he was still not altogether sure why.

CHAPTER 2

It was an odd sensation, waking up on a Monday and not having to go to school. He thought of his father and of the last summer he had lived at home with them. Jason turned over on his back. Thinking of his dad had a tendency to irritate him. Especially when the thoughts involved his mom, too.

That last summer had been the endless summer; endless hours to do nothing but listen to endless fighting. His dad would start the shouting just about this time, too, on his way to work, and resume when he arrived home at night. Perfect timing, Dad, as usual, he thought.

Dad had wanted to move. "Closer to the action, Kiddo," he had said. Great. Chicago. No thanks. And to Jason's surprise his mom had said yes. And no. Yes, Andrew should be closer to the action and should move. No, she and the kids would not. And, by the way, she was filing for divorce. She would have told him sooner, but he had been delayed on business. Andrew had been livid. And so the summer began.

Jason rose with a grunt. He didn't want to think about it. Not then, not now, not later, not ever; and, as he pulled on a pair of gym shorts and headed for the basement, he noticed his mother in the hall just as she noticed him. "Jason," she called. "Garbage detail this morning." "Gotcha," he said, and re-routed his steps to the kitchen. Grabbing the waiting bundle, he noticed the kitchen clock. "Eight-thirty. I must be nuts," he thought, and went out the kitchen door and down the driveway. As he reached the small cluster of cans at the foot of the drive, his eyes caught a flicker of sun on metal and, shielding his eyes, he looked toward it. Coming toward him were two girls, about his age, on bikes. As they neared, he recognized one of them from school.

"Hello, Jason," said a pudgy girl with curly, dark hair, as she brought her bike to stop in front of the driveway. "Hi, Sonia," Jason replied. Jason recognized Sonia from school. It was the other girl, though, that caught his attention. He had never seen her before, but immediately knew that he would want to see her again.

Girls had never held an interest for Jason. The two he had in his life represented opposite ends of the spectrum, and anything in between would have seemed like a cheat to him. At four, Deenie was the ultimate vamp. Just coming into her own, she was seductive, coy, childish, manipulative and yet utterly charming, all in one. His mother, at the other end of the spectrum, was beautiful, warm, tender, and understanding. Next to the females already in his life, the immature, budding woman of his tenth-grade class did not stand a chance.

Nor, he realized, did he. Although only fifteen, Jason held the physique of a man, not a boy. Daily workouts with a weight set in his basement (one of the few worthwhile gifts his father had ever given him) had matured the boy's appearance while an overzealous father had matured his mind well beyond his fifteen years. It seemed as of late, at least to him, that more than his humor was getting noticed around the house.

And so it was (as he realized that all he was wearing were gym shorts), that he got that strange self-conscious feeling again. He had never been a self-conscious person. It just wasn't allowed with a dad like Andrew Coussens. But lately, it seemed to happen more and more. Or maybe, he thought to himself, I just happen to be under-dressed at the wrong times more and more.

"Well, we won't keep you," said Sonia. "I guess you're going to work out or something, huh?" The other girl seemed poised, as if this were the answer she was waiting for. Blonde hair, big blue eyes, slightly pouty, full lips ... as he worked his gaze downward, he noticed a thin strip of a tan belly between her shorts and top, but not before he determined that she had legs nearly as nice as his mom's.

"I'm sorry. I'm Jason. I don't think we've met," Jason said, extending his hand to shake hers.

"Hi, I'm Liz."

He laughed easily. "Liz, that's my mom's name."

The young blonde laughed easily, too. "Well, I'll understand then if you start calling me Mom."

Jason laughed with her and decided then and there that he definitely wanted to see her again.

*   *   *

"Jason ... telephone!"

"Coming, Mom!" he replied. Jason ran down the hall to the kitchen and picked up the phone. As he lifted the receiver, the voice on the other end was hardly one he expected to hear.

"Jason? Hi. It's Liz. Remember me? I met you the other

day with Sonia."

Silence. Jason was frozen, ear to the phone. A small voice commanded him to speak.

"Hello? Are you there?"

The voice inside him became more insistent. Speak, it commanded. Speak now!

"Yes!" Jason blurted, much louder than he had intended. He dialed it down a notch. "I mean, yes. This is Jason."

"Hi."

"Hi."

"Um. How are you? I mean, how was your workout? I mean, you were going to work out, right?"

Jason searched for something witty to say, "Uh, yeah. Great. I mean the workout was great."

Dork, he chastised himself. You sound like such a dork!

"Great! I mean it's great that you had a good workout."

"Great. I mean thanks."

Hell, I don't know what I mean, Jason thought to himself. Stop beating yourself up and think of something, you oaf! Say something!

And just as he shifted his mind into overdrive, looking for something funny to say, he heard her trying to reach him through the fog he called concentration.

"Well, you're probably wondering why I called. You see, I'm new in town, and I don't know many people. There's a dance at the school; you know, one of those summer dances, and Sonia said you were a good dancer, so I was wondering if you were going to go."

"Sure," said Jason.

She paused, and then continued on. "I am really kind of a shy person, although you probably can't tell from this call. It is sort of out of the blue, you know, but I really am shy. I would feel much better if I at least knew ONE guy there that I could dance with. You wouldn't have to dance with me all night or anything; well not unless you wanted to, but I would feel better just KNOWING that I knew someone there, someone that I could dance with if I wanted to."

"I said sure."

"Sure?"

"Yeah, sure."

"You will?"

"Yeah. When is it?"
"Wednesday. Wednesday at seven. Is that okay?"

Jason chuckled, "Sure it's okay. Do you want me to walk you there? I mean, that is if you're going alone."

"I was going to go with Sonia. But why don't you come with us both? I hate to see Sonia go alone. That is, if I went with you."

Jason thought a moment.

"I'll understand if you say no," added Liz, although the drop in her voice told Jason that she hoped that he wouldn't.

Jason sighed. "Tell Sonia to go to your house and I'll walk over and escort you BOTH to the dance. Six thirty on the nose. Sound good?"

Liz's smile beamed through the phone. "Great! Six-thirty. We won't be late!"

Jason chuckled again. "...Great. Oh, and thanks for asking me."

Liz laughed, and without thinking, let slip, "I can't believe I actually called and did."

There was a moment of awkward silence, and then Jason said, "Well, until Wednesday then."

"Yeah, until Wednesday."

Say something, his insides screamed! You have to say something!

"Well, bye then," she said.

"Wait, Liz?"

"Yes?"

"I, um, I'm really glad you did. Call and ask, that is."

"Really? Thanks, Jason."

"Really."

"Well, bye then."

"Bye."

As he hung up the phone, Jason turned to find his mother, arms folded across her chest, watching him from the doorway to the kitchen. As she leaned against the doorjamb, a faint smile played across her lips as she tilted her head slightly to the right.

"Will my son be out late Wednesday, leaving me without the beauty sleep I so desperately need?" Jason's mom liked to joke that gray hair and wrinkles came from not enough sleep due to worrying about one's children. And Jason was usually quick to point out that her children must be angels, since she sported neither. Today, however, he had other thoughts on his mind.

"Mom, why don't you have a boyfriend?"
Liz straightened herself, her expression changing to one of interested amusement. Jason was growing up. She had noticed the signs, had been watching for them, actually. And now it was happening. He was good, too. Never failing to catch her unaware, as he did now.

"If you don't want to talk about it..." he continued.

"No!" Liz interjected. "That's fine. I'd be happy to."

"Okay. Then why?"

"The truth is," Liz started, "I do."

Now it was Jason's turn to look surprised. He would have expected any other answer, but not this one.

"Let's talk in the kitchen," Liz continued, and turned to lead the way. Jason followed, frowning in thought.

"Sit down, Dear," she said, pulling out a chair at the table for him. "Juice?"

"No thanks. How long have you had a boyfriend?'" he shot, eyes flashing.

He was aware of being angry, but didn't know why. Hadn't that been what he wanted? Hadn't that been the point of starting this conversation? He was going to tell his mom she should date people, get out more. So why was he angry?

"It's okay to be angry," he heard her voice through the fog. "Jason, it's okay."

He looked up at her again, unaware that he had looked down at all.

"Why do you look at me like that then?" he snapped.

"Look at you like what?'" Liz replied, somewhat startled.

"When I go to work out, you stare at me!" Jason could feel his voice rising. He was focused now. On her. On his mother. On Liz.

Liz sat down slowly, watching him. She folded her arms on the table and gazed at him, quietly.

"Jason," she started, "I look at you because I love you. You are my son. When I look at you, I can see your pain, your soul. I know how you are... and if you need me... and if I need to wait for you to come to me. Like you have now." She paused, watching him. "Jason, I have a man, a man that I see. He is a wonderful man and I care very much for him. But I care for you more. And for your sister. You have both lived through hell, and I cannot guarantee that another man would not bring that here again. You are, in a sense, my man. The man of this house..."

Jason looked up into her face.

"The only man of this house. Before that, you are my son, and that is sacred."

Jason felt shame clouding his face, drowning the frustration and anger he had felt a moment ago. "I'm sorry, Mom," he choked. And he continued to look at her, as she did at him. Inside, he felt as though he would explode. He wanted to hold her, have her hold him, like it used to be... but somehow he knew those days were over. Or were they?

"It's okay," his mom said again. "I am your mother, and it will always be a mother's right to comfort her son." And then they were standing, clinging to each other.

Jason held her so tight he thought she would break, knowing all along she really would not. And as his mind wandered to an unknown male face, he wondered if his mother held Him like this, and then, in an instant, knew she did not. For he was her son, and she was his alone.

CHAPTER 3

Deenie stood staring into Jason's closet, hands on hips. "The red shirt would go with the brown pants, but it's summer. You just don't wear brown in the summer. The white pants and the pink shirt would look nice."

"This is not Miami, and I am not Don Johnson," interjected Jason, as he came up behind her. His sister watched too much TV, he thought, and he gazed into his closet over her head. She was right, though. Those did appear to be the best combinations.

"What about this," his mother added, entering the room.

Jason turned to her, and followed her as she twisted to pass between them. As she pushed his clothes aside, she pulled out a pair of pleated khaki pants on one hanger and a white ribbed tank on another. A third produced a lime green short-sleeved button down shirt tailored at the waist. She glanced at Jason with a mischievous smile. "These would look nice, and would be seasonal to boot," she added, turning to Deenie.

Jason smiled, letting it grow to a grin. "These would look great!" He took the hangers from his mom. As he admired the outfit, he couldn't help but wonder how it was that she always knew what the best solution was. Like now.

Jason turned to face them. "Now, if you girls don't mind," he sniffed in his tackiest British butler imitation, "I'd prefer to dress in private."

"Why of course," his mom replied, and drawing herself up to be equally as stiff and proper, took Deenie by the shoulders and steered her toward the door. "We do expect first approval rights when you're ready, though," she added, glancing back over her shoulder.

"Why of course," said Jason, and softening his voice, added, "it's the least I owe you." His mother held his gaze for one last moment, and then closed the door behind her.

Once outside the door, Deenie stopped and looked up at her mother. Deep in thought for the past few moments, she could finally contain herself no more. "Why does Jason hide his nice clothes in the back of his closet? He's going to lose them that way."

Liz laughed softly to herself and bent to kiss her young daughter's cheek. "You're right, Dear."

Deenie shook her head and headed for the stairs. "It just seems silly," she said, and if it weren't for the fact that she had to hold the railing as she climbed down the stairs, she would have had her hands on her hips.

As Jason watched the image in the mirror, he could hardly believe his eyes. Was that really him? Since he didn't make it a practice to look at himself in the mirror for long stretches of time, he was somewhat amazed at the man who stared back at him when he finally stepped in front of the glass. He had his mother's blonde hair and crystal blue eyes to compliment and soften the strength of his father's features. Although he had a tendency to look older than his fifteen years, the combination would serve him.

As usual, his mother's taste was impeccable, and the outfit

wore like a dream. Every pleat, every fold, every button was in place, and promised to stay there. Dragging the comb through his bangs one more time, he tried to pull them over and back and then finally settled for the windblown land-where-you-may look he had started with.

Suddenly, as he became aware of the time, or the growing lack of it, he turned to see the clock announcing five past six. Better hustle, he thought to himself, and glancing back at the mirror one last time, he headed into the hall.

Liz glanced at the clock as she helped her daughter pick a color more appropriate for grass than purple. "Try this one, Dear," she said, handing her daughter a grass-green crayon. She sighed as Deenie began coloring the farmer's hair. Smiling broadly, Deenie looked up at her mother and erupted in laughter. "Now he looks like the boys at the mall!" Liz smiled back at her daughter. Deenie's smile faded to a frown, as though she remembered something that had escaped her before, and turned to a fresh, colorless page to color. The new picture was of a large, stately mansion with a small party on the lawn in front. Liz sighed as Deenie colored the grass green.

The sound of steps drew Liz's attention to the foyer outside the kitchen and, although she knew she should try to contain herself, she could not. This was her son's first date, and although he was only fifteen, it never occurred to her to be concerned. Even now as he approached, she felt only pride.

"Well, what do you think?" Jason asked, spinning once before his sister and mother. Deenie glanced up and then continued her coloring.

Liz smiled. "Wow!"

Jason grinned, "You like it?"

"Absolutely fabulous! Will I get you home in one piece?" she teased.

Jason tilted his head in mock scorn, and then leaned forward to kiss her cheek. "I'll be late... gotta run."

As he started away, Liz pulled him back and kissed his cheek in reply. "Have fun, son." She never called him son, and Jason turned to read her thoughts. Satisfied, he smiled and replied, "I will, Mother." He went out the back door and headed down the driveway toward the street.

CHAPTER 4

Walking easily, Jason settled into stride to cover the four short blocks to Liz's house. Up until now, he had managed to keep his nerves at bay. Suddenly, though, they seemed very much alive. He was grateful for the walk and some time to himself.

"Nothing to worry about," he thought to himself, "just a friendly night on the town with some friends." He laughed at the rationalization and it seemed to relax him. He sighed, and as he turned onto Liz's street, he recognized Sonia's figure in the distance hurrying toward Liz's house. He smiled. Late as usual, Sonia. He recalled the class they had together where she had been late more often than not.

As he approached the house, his heart sank. Liz and her parents were sitting on the porch! He slowed his steps to contemplate the situation and, taking a deep breath, turned onto the walk and headed toward them.

Sonia turned to Jason. Red faced and still puffing, she smiled weakly. "Hi, Jason."

"Hello, Sonia," he replied, and then turned his attention to the porch. He extended his hand toward Liz's father. "Good evening, sir."

Somewhat startled, the gentleman scrambled to his feet and, wiping his hand on his pants, extended his own back.

"Ev'nin', son," he said.

As he looked at Jason, he started, as though he seemed to recall something, and then turning to the woman seated in the chair next to him, said, "Oh... this is Marla... and I'm Ed. We're Liz's godparents."

Jason turned to Marla, and leaning toward her, extended his hand.

"Pleased to meet you, Miss Marla," he said, making a mental note to ask Sonia later where Liz's parents lived.
The woman blushed slightly and giggled, "Pleased to meet you!" and glanced about nervously.

Liz took all this in with silent pride, and when it was her turn, she could do no more than blush and drop her eyes to the ground.

"You look very nice tonight, Liz," Jason said, his eyes on her, unaware of his new found power. Liz's blush deepened, and she glanced up only long enough to get out a stifled, "Thank you."

"Where you kids off to tonight?" Ed asked innocently, making conversation. It did not seem to occur to either guardian that they should be concerned, and it was not due to trust either. Ed and Marla had their goddaughter due to no fault of their own, and surely none of Liz's. Her parents had quite suddenly chosen to live in Africa; something to do with a mission or a higher purpose, and so here she was. Ed and Marla had always been fond of the pretty little girl they had were now the spiritual guardians of. They had been surprised, nonetheless, when she had arrived fully grown after a hurried conversation with her parents just three weeks before. Having no children of their own, it had not occurred to them that the passing of some fifteen years since attending her christening would have caused her to grow up. Yet, after the initial shock had worn off, all parties seemed to be adapting well. Marla seemed to be enjoying Liz immensely, and Ed, who had become concerned at Marla's increased lackluster as she commenced in years, was grateful for the new spark Liz seemed to ignite in his wife.

As he waited for a reply, Ed reached over and took his wife's hand, remembering a time long ago when he stood on a porch not much different from this one.

"The high school is having a summer dance," Liz replied. "I thought it would be a good way to get acquainted. And, I heard Jason is a good dancer, so..."
"You don't need to explain, Dear," Ed said with a chuckle, and looking affectionately at his wife, added, "We understand."

"You make a lovely couple," added Marla, as she beamed in Jason's direction. Liz blushed again as Jason gazed her way.

Sonia rolled her eyes and said, "Well, Fred and Ginger, maybe we should head to the dance?"

Now it was Jason's turn to blush, and Liz, recognizing the slight footing she had gained, laughed as she took Sonia's arm and headed down the walkway ahead of Jason.

"Good night, Uncle Ed, Aunt Marla! Liz called. "I won't be home too late!

Jason turned to Ed and said, "It was really nice meeting you," and then to Marla, "Both of you." Marla beamed back at him. "I hope to see you again. Really," Jason added. And he meant it.

Something about this simple couple drew him. They reminded him of a time gone by that he only saw in the movies.

Yet here they were, around the corner from his house, just like in the movies.

"Well, son, you come by anytime now, you hear?" Ed replied, as Jason backed toward the walkway, one eye looking for Liz and Sonia.

"Yes, Dear, anytime! I always have fresh lemonade. And pie! Do you like pie?"

"I love pie!" Jason exclaimed, heading down the walk. And then he stopped. Turning to face Ed and Marla head on, he let intuition take over and spurted out, "Tell you what. I'll bring you berries from the picking farm, and you make the pie. Deal?"

"Oh my!" exclaimed Marla, leaning forward. "That would be wonderful!" And turning to Ed, "Just think! Fresh berry pie, like we used to make!"

Ed turned to Marla, a tear threatening his eye, and then back to Jason.

"Bless you son," he whispered. "Bless you!" And, clearing his throat, "Better run, son; those ladies won't wait forever! Cut a rug!"

Jason smiled and waved, and turned to find Sonia and Liz waiting silently at the head of the walk. Sonia wore a look of disgust and harrumphed as he approached. Liz, though, was smiling softly. A sweet, innocent smile, like one would find on an angel. As Jason reached them, she slipped her arm through his, and, out of earshot of Sonia, breathed, "That was the sweetest thing I've ever witnessed in my whole life. Thank you."

Jason turned to her, his brow wrinkled. "For what?"

Jason looked at her, and then turned away. And then, on second thought, he turned to her again, and with a sheepish grin said, "Does that mean you'll come with me to pick berries?"

CHAPTER 5

Five Star High was only a mile from Liz's house, and the threesome walked the distance in silence. Liz, her arm still through Jason's, walked beside him, with Sonia leading the way. The pace was casual, as neither Jason nor Liz seemed to be in any great hurry, and Sonia had long since given up goading them along. Sonia was beside herself. Somehow, something just wasn't jiving. She had introduced Liz to Jason herself. As far as she knew, since that time, only one phone call had transpired. Just one! And now look at them! She just didn't get it. She would have expected this after the dance, on the walk home. But on the walk there? "Harrumph!" she snorted into the silence, unheard by her followers in the rear.

As the three of them turned into the lane leading to the high school, Sonia skirted ahead. They can find their own way if they don't care to keep up, she thought.

"We'll see you inside," Jason called, as he noticed her slipping away.

Sonia shot him an acid look and walked all the faster.

"I think she's mad," Liz said, looking after Sonia's departing form. "I don't know her all that well, do you?"

"Sure," said Jason, although in fact he realized he didn't know anyone from school all that well. "I had a class with her last year."

Liz laughed, "No, silly. Know her as a *friend*. Talk to her." And then she leaned into Jason, squeezing his arm, and added "Do you know her innermost secrets."

Suddenly uncomfortable, Jason frowned and pulled away. "No, I don't know her that well." Forcing a smile he added, "Well, here we are." They stood staring, alternately looking at the door to the gymnasium and at each other.

With a bang the door flew back and Sonia stepped out onto the walk, "Oh, you're here." Sonia glared at Jason, and then softened her gaze as she turned to Liz. "I have some people I would like you to meet. You did come here to meet people, didn't you? To 'get acquainted, I thought you said?"

"Yes!" Liz said brightly, and turning to Jason, "I'll see you inside, okay?"

"Sure," said Jason, studying Sonia and taking in the glare and the hurt in her eyes.

As Liz and Sonia retreated into the gym, his thoughts drifted back to the realization that he really didn't *know* anyone from school.

"Jase, my man!" came a familiar call. Jason turned to find Scat sauntering toward him and he felt a spontaneous grin stretching across his face.

"Yo bro!" came his reply, as he had done every day since the first day Scat had shown up unexpectedly at Five Star High. He did know someone! And Scat knew him.

'Friends at first sight, in sorrow and delight, forever and a day, true friends shall we stay,' ran through Jason's mind.

It was their motto. They had made it up one rainy afternoon under the bleachers at a rained out baseball game, and it had sealed their friendship forever. Jason and Scat knew more about each other than either knew about themselves.

Scat's family was not unlike most of the Five Star region's new settlers. Discouraged by their more urban lifestyles, and fearful of the various unfiltered influences on their kids, these people migrated to the Five Star region to recapture the nostalgic sense of a "home town" they had all heard existed when their parents were kids. Five Star boasted just such a lifestyle.

Barely on the map, the Five Star region was made up of five small towns. Though each was too small to have any individual claim to fame, together they boasted an excellent high school and junior high school, located just within each town's border. Since the time of their founding, no town had yet grown large enough to encompass the schools' building sites. They were simply called the Five Star Junior High and High School, after the five towns whose children would make up the two student bodies. Although each town had its own flavor, all were similar in that they were modern, they were affluent, and they were diverse with a capital "D." Oh, and they were all smack dab in the middle of scrub and tumbleweed country in the arid southwest. Not quite desert, not quite grass, once you left the manmade borders of each of Five Star's towns, you entered bleak, flat countryside. No one seemed to notice, though. The lawns were beautifully manicured and something was always in bloom in Five Star, no matter what town you lived in.

Scat's story was not unusual for a Five Star kid. A rough and tumble pre-teen from the streets of Chicago, Scat had lived on the edge until two years ago. His mother, widowed when Scat was six, met and married a prominent black investment counselor, and at the age of thirteen Scat found himself moving to the opposite side of the tracks. A few weeks in the new neighborhood told all parties involved that the new living arrangements weren't going to work. Undaunted, and determined not to give up his new family that easily, Scat's stepfather decided that, rather than having two fish out of water, he would make it three. They pulled out the stakes and moved to Liberty Junction, one of Five Star's sister cities. The sign outside the city said, "Welcome to Liberty Junction, Gateway to Paradise!" and Scat's folks had been prepared to believe it.

Scat's mom, Felice, fell in love at first sight. The house, the yard, the flower garden, the trees... she would go on forever, pointing out the things she loved about her new home. His stepfather, Dan, had converted the detached garage out back into his office, and kept his new family close to him like chicks to a hen. Scat, after his first misgivings, decided he could "roll with it," and went off to his new school with the highest of hopes. He knew that somehow this would work out... it had to.

And as he entered his new school—Five Star Junior High School—he saw the kid. Bopping to the beat, sassing to the sound, jamming to the gyro. He quickly learned the others called him Jason. Realizing that this was his gift—his link to sanity in this "paradise," he waited for his chance and then made his move. Sashaying over to Jason, in his loudest, strongest, clearest voice, he made himself known.

"Jase, my man!"

There was silence in the hall. All eyes turned to Scat. Jason stopped his movement and turned to see a tall, lanky black boy with small round spectacles. His teeth flashed "peace," and Jason, so taken aback by the incongruity of the situation, spontaneously grinned back at the boy. Then, turning his back, he looked over his shoulder at the kid and cried "Yo bro!", extended his hand behind his half turned back so the kid could give him a five.

Scat stiffened, startled, and then grinned even wider. With a breathy, "Aw right!" he slapped Jason a five and then melted into a relaxed stance that belied the fact that he had bones. Still grinning, Jason wrinkled his brow in amazement and, nudging Scat along, headed down the corridor with the boy at his side. As they turned the first corner, Jason turned to Scat without breaking stride and breathed under his breath, "Who are you?"

"Scat-man's my name, scat is my game!" announced Scat, pirouetting down the hall in a series of boneless spins. Jason laughed and shook his head.

"But seriously," Scat continued, "you got style, man. And style is something that we can't live without. If you got it, you got to be with it, or you drown. You know what I mean, man?"

Jason knew all too well what the boy was talking about, and his grin faded as he turned to stare at the boy.

"What do you want from me?" Jason asked in a low tone.

Throwing up his hands and stepping back, Scat clarified himself. "Yo dude, nothing *from* you. Just friends, man. That's all. Just friends."

And relaxing, Scat continued, "I'm new, you're not. Just friends." And as Scat's gumption started to fade, he dropped his eyes. "Aw, forget it. Sorry to bother you," and he turned to go.

"Wait," came the low sound; barely audible. Thinking out loud, Jason continued. "You're definitely a little rough around the edges, but you're harmless."

Scat looked up, surprised.

"I mean, you're not dangerous or anything." Jason dug the

hole deeper. "Look, yeah, you're right on some counts, but you're a bit... abrupt. Yeah, abrupt. That's all. You sort of startled me. But yeah, sure, I'd like to be friends."

And now it was Scat's turn to wrinkle his brow, despite the grin that was spreading across his face.

And so it grew, their friendship and the town. Junior High to High School, and now here to the dance. They traveled through time, together, yet apart. Scat had heard that Jason might be at the dance tonight and he was eager to dance. It had been a long time since the two friends had seen each other.

Scat—as a dance style—holds no boundaries. It is an expression of friendship and of war, love and of hate, of purpose and of purposelessness. For Five Star, Jason and Scat's dancing was just that: "Expression." For them, it was their connection to each other's soul as well as their own.

CHAPTER 6

Liz followed Sonia through the side door into the thin crowd. It was still early and the "fashionably lates" hadn't arrived yet. Sonia began weaving her way toward the back wall, glancing occasionally over her shoulder to see if Liz still trailed behind her.

"The decorations are great," Liz exclaimed, trying to make conversation. Getting no response, she began searching the groups they passed for a friendly face. She was starting to get that sinking feeling again, the same feeling she had gotten when her best friend in Chicago had taken her to a "meeting" that turned out to be a Moonie recruitment session. Something didn't seem right here, and as they approached a group of girls, one blowing huge bubbles with a wad of pink gum, Liz realized that her intuition was going to be right... again.

"Hi, Carol!" crooned Sonia, frisking about the group of girls like a love-starved puppy. Having pretended not to notice her approach, Carol was now forced to acknowledge Sonia's presence, which she did with an exaggerated, annoyed stare. Turning her head slowly, she glared at Sonia with a "what-do-you-want" look that commanded that whatever Sonia's answer was, it had better be a good one.

Undaunted, Sonia replied, "This is Liz. She's new in town and I told her I'd help her get acquainted." Sonia beamed at Carol, searching her face for a sign of approval.

Carol turned her head slowly toward Liz, taking her in from head to foot. A quizzical look softened her face, replacing the glare, and then gradually settled to one of puzzled surprise.

Just then, a tall, slender girl stepped from behind the group and, taking Liz by the elbow, introduced herself and steered Liz away.

"Hi, I'm Amanda. You can call me Andy though. I know, it's silly, but it's better than the regular string of cliché names you get from 'Amanda'."

Liz was grateful for Andy's bantering and let herself be led away from Sonia and the other girls. Andy seemed friendly, and she "felt" friendly.

"Want some punch? It's good stuff," Andy continued, and headed them toward the buffet table.

Safely out of earshot of the others, punch glasses in hand, Andy sobered her demeanor and looked hard at Liz.

"How did you hook up with Sonia?" she asked, just as puzzled as Carol had been.

"We live near each other and we sort of met on the street one day," Liz answered, seeing no particular reason not to tell her. "She offered to introduce me around, and this dance seemed like a logical starting place."

Andy nodded, and stared in her punch. "Hard facts –" she began, raising her eyes and staring firmly at Liz, "the group of girls

Sonia was introducing you to were not a 'nice group of girls'. They are, nonetheless, the 'in-group of girls'. There's a big difference."

Liz nodded, focusing on what she was hearing.

"You seem like a 'nice girl'. I am a 'nice girl', and that's a lot of why we're standing here now. I know them. I hang in their wings, but I am not one of them. Do you understand the difference?"

"I think so," Liz whispered in a far off tone.

"You need to *know* so," said Andy, "or you will get eaten. Eaten alive." Andy stared off, seeming to remember something, and then snapping back, continued. "You need to know so. Let's get it clear..."

"I know the difference," Liz interjected, the sudden harsh tone in her voice throwing both of them off guard. Andy glanced around casually, and then refocused on Liz.

"Call me a Good Samaritan, if you will. Like attracts like, and that's the truth." Laughing softly, she then said, "Welcome to Five Star High."
Liz laughed too, although inside she felt like crying. She thought of Africa, as she always did in moments like this, and wondered what there could possibly in this world that was worse.

The two girls stood with each other, each lost in thought. Andy was the first to be distracted by the noise on the dance floor, partly because she recognized it and associated it with something she held dear. Smiling, Andy touched Liz's arm. "Let's go meet some *real* nice people," Andy said gently to Liz, careful to be sensitive of any adverse impact their previous conversation may have left.

Liz drifted back through her thoughts to Andy and smiled back. "Sure," she chirped, and laughing, added, "I think I like my odds better this time."

Andy's eyes glistened. She felt that as a special compliment, and somehow she knew her perception was not off. Liz was a special girl. How they had managed to find one another in Five Star was not important; only where they took their friendship from here.

The two girls wound their way through the crowd to the dance floor. There, amid the crush of bodies, Andy and Liz strained for a glimpse of the excitement emanating from the floor ahead. Andy frowned slightly and looked around for a better position. Turning to Liz, she shouted above the crowd, "I think they just started!"

Liz turned to Andy, shouting in an effort to be heard over the din. "Who just started what?"

With a knowing smile, Andy waved Liz through the crowd to the left and shouted back, "You'll see!"

The two girls clamored up the side stairs to the gymnasium's stage and, skirting the DJ's booth, found seats on the narrow ledge above the dance floor. From this perch, they could see clearly the two whirling bodies slightly below them.

"That's Jason!" Liz screamed at Andy and into the din.

Andy turned to Liz, "You know Jason?!"

"Yes, I came with him... sort of."

Andy's face held a puzzled look for a moment and then she broke into a grin. "I knew you were a nice girl!"

Liz laughed, and turning back to the dance floor, realized her unspoken question had gone unanswered.

Scat and Jason had entered the gym almost immediately upon hooking up. The crowd of kids inside was growing steadily and both were eager to get things moving. A few brave souls shimmied about the dance floor, but for the most part they would have the floor to themselves. Scat moseyed toward the DJ for a pep talk as Jason stripped off his outer shirt. He spun easily on a heel and slid to the right, watching Scat's progress through the crowd. The crowd had begun pressing toward the floor as word of Jason and Scat's presence made its way through the gym. Dancing in the halls at school was one thing, but dancing for real was a sight to see and no one wanted to miss out.

As the music ended, the DJ switched to a livelier tempo and Scat, having found his way to Jason's side, shrugged and feigned indifference to the bad selection.

"He said he'd give it his best shot," Scat said. "Guess we'll have to work around it."

Jason grinned, "I do my best work working around it," and he stepped to the edge of the floor. He and Scat waited there, poised, chatting idly and letting the music infuse them.

Jason could feel it pulsing into him, up through his feet and into his legs, and he began to move. At first the movement was barely perceptible, but as it coursed up his legs and into his spine, he let the waves of rhythm carry him. Before he was even aware that it was happening, he was free. Sliding, spinning, moving... forever moving. In and out of the sound; with it, around it, coaxing it, cajoling it, expressing each note in infinite detail. He was free.

And with him was Scat, the same, yet infinitely unique, expressing his interpretation of the same sounds in the same instant; with him, against him, around him and within him. They were poetic, yet stark all at once, neither displaying form nor formlessness, meaning nor meaningless. They were pure expression, yet they expressed only that which the viewer chose to see. They were soul, and the soul's window within.

They danced like this, Scat and Jason, to the awe of the crowd, for some three to four songs. Alone, each putting forth his experience for all to see, all to feel, they at last began to wind down. Not tired, but spent. As the bolder kids began to trickle to the floor to join the fun, Jason and Scat moved toward the sidelines, spinning and sliding in smaller and smaller spaces. Out of nowhere, a small, freckled girl with a mane of red hair appeared and carried Scat out onto the floor with her. Scat did not fight her, and the friends knew their time together was over for that evening. Their dancing had become a ritual, and with all rituals, each joyful new beginning was followed by the bittersweet taste of closure.

Jason watched Scat with his new partner and chuckled aloud. Scat always managed to find the ones who couldn't dance, poor guy, and as he started to scan the floor for a partner of his own, she caught his eye. She was watching him intently from a seat on the stage just in front of the DJ's booth. As Jason moved closer, he recognized both their smiles.

"Liz, I see you found a new friend," Jason said, pleased to see Liz sitting with Andy.

"Hi Jason," Andy crooned, and as Jason turned to smile her way, added, "How attached is Scat to his red-headed friend? Would he mind if I stole him for a spin around the floor?"

Jason laughed, "Mind?! He'd be ecstatic!"

Andy laughed, and squeezing Liz's arm whispered, "If you need me I won't be far."

Liz whispered, "Thanks," as Andy dropped the four feet to the gym floor and, with a wave, headed off in the direction of Scat and the red mane.

"Feel like dancing?" Jason asked, and as he looked up into

her face he noticed again all the reasons he first found Liz to be beautiful.

"I thought you'd never ask," Liz kidded, and, extending her arms to him, waited for help down. Jason reached up and gently took her waist and, as she rested her hands on his shoulders, he lifted her down. Liz was overcome with the intense feeling that she was floating and, as her feet touched the ground, could do nothing but gaze up into Jason's face with her hands still on his shoulders.

At this close proximity, Jason felt the beginnings of a cold sweat. His own face barely twelve inches from hers, he had the most intense desire to just reach down and kiss her. No one would notice; just reach down. She was waiting, yet she wasn't. To him, Liz seemed trapped in her own feelings, yet trapped in his at the same time. They were one, yet not. Maybe they were two trying to become one. That was it! If he would just kiss her, that would do it, they would be one. They would each come back to here... from there...

He leaned toward her, barely six inches from her face, from her lips.

... And they would be together here, not wherever they both were, wherever they both had gone.

And as Liz's eyes cleared, she saw him, barely six inches from her face, and she sighed. He saw her, too, and it made him want her more. And he bent his head gently, and just before his lips grazed hers, he whispered, "May I kiss you?" And as Liz parted her lips to reply, she felt his upon hers, and answered him with her soul instead.

Her lips were warm, so very warm, and as he gently pulled them away from hers, the depth of her eyes called him back. Again he kissed her, harder this time, his tongue exploring the space between her lips. She seemed to melt, to become part of him, so that where he ended and where she started no longer was discernible. Two bodies, two souls. Two, yet one; fused, yet separate.

Jason lifted his lips from hers and buried his face in the blonde hair at her neck. He hugged her, unaware of when his hands had left her waist and come to rest around her, cradling her. Liz sighed, resting her cheek on his shoulder as her fingers toyed with the curls at the back of his neck.

It seemed like a lifetime had passed in one, powerful, amazing moment, ending only when the two raised their heads and looked at one another again. Sheepishly, Jason grinned, "I've never done anything like this before. I'm sorry if I offended..."

Liz placed her finger over Jason's lips. "No. It takes to two do something like this, and I was here too."

Jason looked hard at her and frowned slightly. "Where? I mean, how do you know these things?"

Liz laughed lightly. "That is a long conversation and not much fun. Tonight, we have fun. Deal?"

"Deal," Jason replied, with a nod of his head, and tightening his grip around her waist, lifted her off the ground and spun her, around and around and around. "How's that for a whirl around the dance floor?" he laughed, as Liz, eyes shining and head thrown back, laughed too.

Andy found Scat in the far corner of the gym. He appeared suddenly from the shadows as she was turning to work her way up the far wall. He took her arm and steered her back into the crowd, melting them both from view.

"Took you long enough," he whispered.

Andy laughed. "Well, no strings are no strings."

Andy and Scat had been an item, on and off, and Andy still liked stacking the deck when she could. No one knew what had finally ended things, other than that friendships shouldn't always be more than just that -- friendships.

Scat glared at her, but her spirit was infectious and he leaned over and kissed her cheek. Andy turned to him and smiled. Some things would never change; could never change.

"Where's Jason?" Scat asked. "Let's bug outta' here."

Tradition commanded that friends gather at the lake after formal school functions, so going home often entailed instigating a migration. Scat had had enough of the dance, so the lake was the next stop.

"There he is," Andy said, nodding toward the stage, "dancing with Liz."

"Good, grab him and let's go," Scat pushed, eager to be out the door.

Andy frowned in thought, and turning to Scat said, "Why don't you head outside? We'll meet you by the door, okay?"

Scat started to agree and then stopped himself. "What are you up to?" he growled, trying to peer around her. "I think I'll just go with you, thanks."

Andy bounced around in front of him for a moment, but she was no match for his height. She could tell when he stopped moving that he had seen for himself.

Jason and Liz danced easily, hand in hand, chatting together. Occasionally he'd spin her around or guide them through a sequence of salsa steps, but for the most part they just swayed to the music. Neither the shift in the crowd nor the change in the beat had much effect on either of them, so when Andy appeared next to them, Jason barely noticed her.

"Andy!" Liz said, more to Jason and herself than to Andy.

Jason turned to look at her and smiled. "Find Scat?"

"Yeah, she found me," came the thick reply. Scat moved up next to Andy and into view. Jason stiffened, sensing the tension in Scat's voice, and then relaxed. Old stuff, he thought to himself, old stuff.

"Not that old, man," Scat breathed, and then turning to Andy, added, "Lake time."

Jason looked at Andy. She shrugged. "I'm walking Liz home," Jason said, as though that was the answer. Scat turned to Jason, the anger gone as suddenly as it had come. "Ten minutes. Ten minutes at the lake. No more."

Jason sighed.

"We need this," Scat continued. His voice dropped to a whisper. "I need this... to apologize."

Jason's eyebrows shot up. Andy watched him, expectantly, and then turned to Liz. Liz stood quietly, still grasping Jason's hand.

Odd, Andy thought, it seems I've never known them apart. No, that's not it... like I've never known one without the other being there. No... Oh, hell. I don't know.

And as Andy struggled with her thoughts, Jason moved the small band toward the door. Liz no longer held his hand, but walked easily before him next to Andy. Scat had dropped in beside Jason. Neither boy said a word as each man collected his thoughts.

CHAPTER 7

"Do you hear it?" Jason whispered, his cheek brushing Liz's hair.

The four of them were perched on the Lookout, a broad, flat rock that overlooked the lake. Their backs to Five Star proper, in front of them stretched a large, inky black lake. Beyond the lake stretched acres and acres of rolling green fields as far as the eye could see.

"Hear what?" Liz questioned, leaning back against Jason's shoulder.

They were seated on the rock, gazing out over the water. A breeze had picked up and Jason could faintly make out the sound of horses whinnying in the distance.

"The horses," Jason said, his tone still hushed; "I think they're getting ready to run."

Liz looked up at him quizzically, "I didn't know there were horses around here," she said.

Jason smiled at her. "There aren't."

Horse Valley got its name from its original inhabitants – the horses. Legend had it that in the early Thirties, a wealthy land mogul came to the area and bought both the lake and its surrounding area for his prize horses. He turned it into a sanctuary for all forty of them, and let them loose to thrive in the land's lush fields. Gradually, though, the horses began to sicken and die. Although the man had their bodies examined, the cause of their deaths was never determined. After losing most of his herd within just a few months, he finally gave up and took the remaining animals away with him, leaving the land to nature. To this day, when the wind blows through the trees around the lake, you can distinctly hear whinnying in the distance. The townspeople say it's the herd of dead horses whinnying as they race through the fields, looking for their master who left them behind. And odder still, since the mogul left, the fields around this lake have never become overgrown, although no animals were ever seen grazing on them. The land stayed just as it had always been: pastures surrounding a lake.

"...and that's the legend," Andy said, looking from Scat to Liz. Scat had heard the story many times before, but he had never seen the horses themselves. He still found it hard to swallow. Jason had seen them once before, or thought he had, and he believed the legend literally. Tonight he had that odd feeling again that the horses were there. It was the same feeling he had had the first time he thought he saw them, except that night it had rained hard and he was well down the path toward the road when he heard the cries in the night. He had been with Andy, and she had dragged him back up to the ledge in time to see the tiny forms streaking into the trees at the far side of the north shore.

Now he was here again and he could feel it; feel the energy. The air crackled with it, and he was sure. He had seen them then and he would see them now, and with that realization he turned deliberately toward the lake and the open space beyond.

Andy smiled to herself and turned to Liz. "Let's go back to the top rock," she said. "We can see better from there."

Jason nodded. "Yeah, we'll join you in a minute."

Scat watched the girls as they rose out of sight, up the path. Then he sighed. The horse talk went with the territory and he refused to let it get to him. Not tonight. He had more important things on his mind than to argue about dead horses.

Andy knew just about everything there was to know about the legend, and what she didn't know she found a way to find out. When Andy had finally relayed the story to Jason, Jason started talking about it too and Scat had teased him, saying he had 'swallowed it, hook, line and sinker.' But the legend was a bonding point, and it had deepened Jason and Andy's friendship considerably. For the most part, Scat saw Jason's interest as serving as a buffer, but he knew now that that buffer had been one he was both grateful for and jealous of. And now, as tonight, as Liz got her first history lesson on the lake, Scat felt the old wounds working their way open again. It was fine that he didn't believe in the legend, and neither Andy nor Jason had bothered him about it when he made it clear that he wasn't interested. But it still left him out. Like when he would call their houses and neither would be home. "At the lake," their mothers would say. And he would be alone, left to wonder.

The breeze lifted the hair from Jason's forehead and he turned to Scat.

"You wanted to talk..." he started, unsure if he should push on or let it die. Something had been bothering Scat for a while and, as usual, it seemed to center around Andy. Tonight, though, had a different flavor to it, and Jason was curious to see what Scat had on his mind.

"Yeah," Scat muttered, collecting his thoughts and trying to push the prancing ponies out of his mind. "I do."

He rubbed his hand over the short nap on his head. Smooth and tight, his mind whispered, and he smiled. Andy had always liked running the palm of her hand over his head, except she had always used 'smooth and tight' to refer to something else. He chuckled aloud and shook his head. "Yeah, let's talk."

Jason frowned and turned back toward the lake. The wind picked up and rustled the leaves on the trees. Jason watched them as they danced on their stems. Strong and robust, it would be months before the wind would blow them loose. As the leaves began to slow from their frenzied dance, he heard it -- long, low moaning neighs echoing over the lake, sharp and clear.

"What the hell was that?" whispered Scat. He had come to Jason's side and was squatting beside him. Whatever it was, he didn't want it seeing him. At least not standing there, alone.

Jason turned to him, eyes bright, and whispered: "The horses."

Scat looked at Jason from the corner of his eye and wished he were home, where dream horses stayed in your dreams.

Liz and Andy climbed down to the edge of the lake and then tilted up their faces to the night air. They scanned the rocks above for signs of life, trying to pick out the ledge where Scat and Jason sat, but with no luck. It was from this vantage point that they heard the neighs and felt the shudder in the air as the sound echoed over the lake.

Liz moved closer to Andy, looking about her as though the air were alive. She didn't like this and turned to Andy to tell her so.

"Maybe we should go back," Liz said, barely whispering.

"We told the guys we were going to the top rock." Andy seemed not to notice and started picking her way through the blackness toward an indiscernible destination. Liz looked forlornly toward the path they had come on and then fell in behind Andy. "Where are we going?" she whispered.

"To the field," Andy replied.

"The field? What field?" Liz asked, stopping short.

"The field where the horses begin their run," Andy replied, matter-of-factly, as though this was something she did every day. Actually, it was just something she had always wanted to do, and now seemed the time to go for it. The timing is perfect, Andy thought to herself. Jason will understand, and he'd do the same. Focusing her attention on the trail ahead, Andy ducked her head and headed into the reeds.

Liz turned on her heel and without a sound, made her way back to the trail. Within moments she found herself on the overlook and as she headed down the short path to where she and Andy had left Scat and Jason, she was surprised to see them rushing up the path toward her.

"Liz!" Scat whispered loudly.

Startled, Liz looked from Jason to Scat questioningly. The night's events were beginning to take their toll on her and an air of incredulity was beginning to shroud her world.

Jason took Liz by the shoulders and held her. "Where's Andy, Liz?" Jason whispered, although he knew the answer. He and Scat had been scanning the fields, watching for movement when they had seen Andy pop out of the reeds mid-field. From above you could tell that the lake was not the starting point of any run, but the mid-point and the last leg to the forest. Andy was in the way of anything that would or would not travel through that stretch of field.

"Stay here with Scat, Liz," Jason said.

"I ain't staying here!" Scat hissed.

"Yes you are!" Jason shot back. His tone was firm. "You don't know this area at night and I do. I'll be back with Andy in a few minutes."

Jason turned and headed down the path to the lake's edge. "Damn you, Andy," he muttered to the air. They had promised each other no funny business. No one, not either of them, was to try to see the horses up close. It was too dangerous. They didn't know what they were looking for or where to see it, so they had both agreed not to try anything foolish. And now this. No wonder Scat went crazy with her.

Once he had arrived at the edge of the lake, Jason headed toward where he thought Andy would go. As he made his way through the long grass, he felt a distinct chill in the air, as though it were getting cooler the further he got from the lake. When he suddenly tumbled through the last stand of reeds and into the field, Jason was taken aback. Heavy swirls of mist covered the field. It seemed to be coming from all around him and moving toward the lake.

"Andy! Where are you!" Jason called, looking around him, trying to pierce through the thick mist. With the air so thick, he was reluctant to move about aimlessly.

"Jason, over here!" came the reply.

"Stay put, I'm coming!" he answered, already moving in the direction of the voice.

It took less than a minute for the two to connect, and Andy's sheepish look told Jason that she was having second thoughts about where she was and what she wanted to do.

"Don't be mad, Jason," Andy said. "I didn't mean anything. It just seemed so right..."
"Forget it, let's get out of here," Jason replied, looking for a likely path through the reeds.

"I'm puzzled, though," Andy added. "When I came through the reeds there was no mist in the fields. Now it's like pea soup out here. What do you make of it?"

Jason wished he could say, "Nothing. That's just nature for you," but he knew that was not the case. The sudden appearance of the mist had intrigued him too.

"I don't know, but I can tell you this: If we don't get out of here, we're in for some trouble. So let's go."

And then they heard it. A cry; loud and guttural. What had been a soft, haunting moan from the direction of Overlook was now a piercing scream. Andy and Jason looked at one another, paralyzed. And then they heard it—the rumble, like distant thunder.

"Let's go!" Jason screamed, grabbing Andy's arm and steering them back toward the tall grass. Andy pulled away, freeing herself, and moved away from him along the edge of the field. Jason stared after her in disbelief. Just ahead was the base of the rock outcropping that Overlook was perched on. The path back up rose along the rocky bank of the dark lake. So why was Andy heading in the opposite direction? She moved like a robot, automatic in her motions and her purpose, and Jason wondered if she knew what she was doing. Should he stop her? Or should he follow her?

Suddenly, Andy jerked, shifting back to reality. She turned and covered the short distance back to Jason's side and this time she grabbed *his* arm. "Quickly," she hissed, "we haven't much time."

The two of them covered the short distance to a craggy outcropping of rock amid the rumble of hooves. The sound was deafening, and as they reached the outer edge of the hard, crumbling surface, they flattened themselves against the rock wall, hand in hand.

The animals seemed to come from everywhere. Large, small, thick, thin; all a dusty gray-black in color. Manes and tails flying, they raced out of the mist, seeming to materialize from nothing, but definitely having come from somewhere. The wind rushed about them, filling their flared nostrils and giving them speed, but to Jason's surprise the animals weren't running toward anything! They ran in a circle -- one ever-widening circle. Around and around they ran as more joined them, materializing out of the wind and the mist.

Jason began to relax, enough at least to try and see what was going on. He edged his head over the rocky outcrop, and saw that the horses were still running, but in a larger circle, as though they were being herded. But by what?

The mist swirled about them, their legs churning the wispy clouds to a froth. Jason looked over at Andy. She had flattened herself against the wall, her arms over her face to shield her eyes. Jason smiled, and pushed himself away from the wall to see if he couldn't get a better look at the swirling mass. It seemed that several of the horses had lost some of their definition, and he wasn't sure if his eyes were playing tricks on him or not. As they flew by though, he could swear they seemed to glance his way, or cock an ear in his direction.

And then as quickly as they had come, they were gone.

Jason had taken two steps away from the wall when, like shooting stars in the night, the gray whirling mass was gone. But where? The mist had shredded into faint wisps, the horses were gone, and Andy and he were alone again.

The silence in the air was almost unbearable. Andy peeked over the top of her arm to see Jason standing a few steps ahead, staring into the distance. She pulled herself upright and walked over to him. He turned as she approached. "You okay?" he asked.

Andy smiled thinly. "Been better."

Jason turned back to the field and focused on the distance. "How did you know? he asked into the air.

"Hmm?" Andy responded, puzzled at the question. "How did I know what?"

"The reeds," Jason answered. "How did you know not to go into the reeds?"

Andy looked blank. Her face paled a little.

Jason continued when Andy said nothing. "I wanted us to go into the reeds and you stopped us. How did you know?" Jason had turned to face her and was watching her eyes intently.

Andy looked at the ground, frowning. "I didn't know. At least I'm not aware that I knew. It was sort of an impulse."
"An impulse," Jason repeated, and then sighed. He looked up toward Overlook and thought of Scat and Liz. They were waiting. "Let's go. Scat and Liz are waiting. Let's see if they saw something too."

Andy snapped her head up. "You saw something!"

"Sure. I had my eyes open." Jason knew the remark would hurt, but that was her fault. It had been her idea and she hadn't even seen what she had come to see.

Andy looked nervous. "Yeah, let's go," she said and started around the rocks.

Jason shook his head. "Women," he muttered.

Andy stiffened at the remark, but kept quiet. She had a bad feeling about this. No one had ever seen the horses before. Yeah, she had a bad feeling about this alright. .

As they rounded the rocks, they ran into Liz and Scat coming the other way. "Jason!" Liz called, trying to mask the relief in her voice. "Where did you guys run off to?"

Andy and Jason looked at each other.

"What do you mean?" Jason replied, puzzled.

Liz laughed, "Is this a game? Well, okay. We saw you come through the reeds about fifty feet down field from Andy, and then you went toward her and joined her. Then you both started walking this way, and then we lost you. We waited a while, figuring you were coming this way, but then we decided we'd better look for you. So, where did you guys run off to?"

Jason and Andy looked at each other, and then Andy turned to Liz. "You didn't see any mist from up there, on the field or around the lake?"

Scat and Liz exchanged glances. "Well," Scat started, "it sort of looked like a veil or something was blocking our view, it could have been mist, so that's why we came down. We thought maybe you got lost."

Jason looked at Andy again and then back to Scat.

"It made sense when it was happening," Scat muttered.

"I know what you mean, man," Jason added, and the two boys looked at one another. "I wish I understood one-third of this," Scat said.

Jason glanced at Liz. She was staring off into the distance, as though she could see something and had been looking at it for a while. Andy noticed her and whispered, "Don't do that. You're giving me the creeps."

Liz didn't say a word, but lifted her hand and pointed into the distance. Scat saw them first and, clenching his teeth to keep his jaw from dropping open, hissed, "Jesus!" through his teeth. Andy and Jason turned and followed the line of Liz's finger with their eyes. There in the distance watching them was a herd of gray-black horses.

"Oh my God," Andy said, barely audible, but loud enough for the rest to hear. Jason grabbed Liz's hand out of the air and held it tight. Liz, startled, looked at him, and then noticing what it was she had pointed at, covered her mouth with her other hand and crushed herself against Jason's side. "I'm scared, Jason," she said.

"I know. Me too," came his reply. Looking into her eyes, he pulled himself up tall and added, "Everything's going to be okay. They're just horses."

"Jason, can I see you a minute?" came Andy's voice, soft and faltering.

It was not like her, at all, Jason thought. He kissed Liz's forehead and said to her, "Two minutes. I'll be right back. Don't move." Then he turned to Scat and added, "Either of you."

Andy and Jason had just moved out of earshot when Andy turned and, grabbing Jason by the back of the neck, pulled his ear to her mouth and hissed, "What did you see?"

Jason jerked back, frowning. "What the hell...!" he started, and then, as if suddenly aware of prying eyes around him, dropped his voice. "What's your problem?!"

"What's my problem?" Andy mocked. "My problem is that we have a herd of ghost horses standing there staring at us when before we couldn't even get a glimpse of them. How's that for a problem?"

Jason watched her, waiting. No use arguing, he thought.

Andy glared at him, and then as suddenly as she had grown angry, she softened into her old self again. She looked at the ground and, after a deep breath, raised her eyes to Jason again. "You okay?" he asked.

"Jason, what have we gotten them into?" she asked. She glanced at the herd again and sighed.

And then she began again, keeping her eyes on the herd, talking to no one. Her words were aimed toward anyone who was listening. Deep in thought, she spoke, as though the words came from somewhere deep in her subconscious.

"According to legend, the herd obeyed only its master. They are here running around the lake in some sort of bizarre ritual looking for their lost master. It would seem that when you saw them, Jason, they also saw you. You acknowledged them and now they seem to be acknowledging you. It would then logically follow that they now think you are their master."

Jason looked again toward the herd. They were milling about, but more in a waiting state than anything else. And worst of all, when he looked at them, they stilled, as though they knew, as though they were expecting something. Something from him.

Andy continued. "Since no one has come near them in forty or so years, that would make sense." And, as though to affirm her thoughts, she turned to Jason.

The starkness of her gaze startled him. "That's crazy," he said, although he didn't believe it for a minute.

"I hope so," Andy said. "I'm just throwing it out there." And glancing back at the herd she added, "They really are giving me the creeps, though. I wish they'd stop. Funny, isn't it? We spend all this time wishing we could see them. Now we finally do and we want them to go away." Andy smiled despite herself, but it was a shaky smile.

"Well," Jason said in an effort to own some of what was happening, "what if I scare them away?" He knew the moment he said it that it was a dumb idea.

Andy looked at him and added, as though she could read his mind. "No, but you could send them away!"

"Send them away?" Jason asked.

"Yes!" Andy exclaimed. "Tell them to run free."

"Oh sure," Jason snapped. He looked at the herd and with a wave of his arms, as though shooing chickens in a barnyard, he yelled, "Hey guys, mind running free now? Well, go ahead, now's your chance! Run free!"

Andy moved to stop him, but it was too late. Jason's sudden movement toward the herd interrupted her. As suddenly as he had begun the sarcastic gesture, he stopped it. He turned to Andy, his face pale, and whispered the obvious. "They're gone!"

CHAPTER 8

Much to his surprise, Jason awoke at eight-thirty the next morning. As he lay in bed, bits and pieces of the night before played across his mind. When the foursome had finally left the lake and arrived at Liz's house, they had all been surprised to find it was only twelve-thirty. That meant they had been at the lake for only one hour! Andy had puzzled over that fact all the way to the corner where she, Jason and Scat traditionally split company. From there Scat continued on with Andy and walked her to her house. Jason walked alone the two blocks to his own house. Jason guessed Andy had pondered about the time displacement thing until far into the night. "She must be coming up blank," he thought. Jason knew if Andy had thought of something in the night she would have called him by now.

"Jason!" his mother called. "You have company!"

Jason frowned and rolled out of bed. Eight forty-five. It was awfully early for company.

As he planted his feet on the ground and began to rise, his mother appeared in the doorway. Silently she stepped into the room and clicked the door shut behind her. She looked at her son and a chill came over Jason. "Your father is here," she said.

Having half risen, Jason allowed himself to sink gently back to the bed. He watched his mother from this seated position as she came and sat beside him.

"He got in last night. He insisted on waiting for you, but when you weren't back by twelve, he went back to the inn." Liz stared at the floor as she spoke. She seemed distracted, as though she were trying to listen to some far off conversation while continuing her own.

"He would like for you to go to Chicago with him for the summer." Liz paused. Finally, she raised her eyes and looked into Jason's face. With a soft laugh she continued, "Doesn't that sound like fun?"

Jason laughed also and, shaking his head, stated flatly, "No, not at all."

Liz didn't appear surprised and in reality she was not. She knew her son would not want to go and she didn't blame him.

"I'm missing something here," Jason said. "I don't want to go. You would rather have me here. So why the face? What's going on?"

Liz looked at the floor again, a sad smile on her lips. Then she looked Jason in the eye. "Your father prides himself in getting his way. He made it very clear last night that he came here with two plane tickets, so two people *will* return to Chicago. He and one of his offspring; that he made very clear." Liz paused to collect herself and then continued. "He has two children, Jason, and Deenie has already made it quite clear that she would *love* to go."

Jason's jaw dropped. "What!"

Liz shrugged.

"And you'd let her!"

"He is her father. He has every right to visit her and have her visit him."

"Mom..."

"No, he has a right to get to know his children. Providing that, of course, they also want that. I would not make you visit him, yet nor would I refuse you if you wished to visit him."

"Mom..."

"Those are the rules I am comfortable with." Her voice had taken on a slight tremor, and her last comment ended in a squeak.

"Look at me, Mom."

Liz, although facing him, had avoided her son's eyes from the very beginning. She now forced her gaze to meet his and she felt a sudden rush of warmth.

"Don't add my anger to your own, Jason. It would not be fair. You have learned of your own anger and that is more than enough for you."

Jason met his mother's gaze easily. He always felt the most comfortable looking into her eyes. From that perspective he could usually better understand what she was feeling. Tonight though, she was an open book, and Jason began to get confused by the bombardment of juxtaposed emotions that whirled in his mother's eyes.

"Deenie is young. She is actually quite like your father, you know. She should have a wonderful time."

"You're afraid."

Liz laughed, "Terrified!"

"That she won't want to come back?"

Liz snorted. "That she'll want to come back too soon!"

Jason laughed again. As their laughter died, Jason started again, but with a more serious tone. "Really, mom, what is it?"

Liz's smile faded. "I don't know, I just have a bad feeling about this."

Jason shrugged, and grinning broadly, put his arm about his mother's shoulders. "Think of it as a vacation." With that Jason rose and began to look for clothes.

Five minutes later, Jason came down the stairs to say hello to his father. As usual, his father was on the phone.

The night before, Andrew Coussens had arrived at his ex-wife's house to surprise his kids with a visit. His son was out – a date he was told – so he waited. And waited. And grew angrier and angrier. He was not accustomed to waiting, for anyone. As he listened to the airline clerk rattling off flight times, he considered asking Jason anyway. He had been furious at having to wait, and from that anger he was re-ticketing an adult ticket to that of a child. He and his daughter would be flying back to Chicago at four that afternoon. No, he thought, one was enough...

Andrew caught sight of his son and smiled broadly and waved. Jason smiled and waved back, disappearing into the kitchen. Deenie sat at the table, spooning milk and cereal into her mouth one flake at a time, her feet kicking wildly under the table. Jason smiled. His mother was probably right. Deenie would have a great time.

"Jason!" boomed Andrew. "How are you?" Andrew clapped Jason on the back and squeezed the back of his neck.

"Hi, Dad," Jason returned. He turned to face his father.

"I guess you've heard the news. Deenie is coming with me

for a visit. Hey, I'd love to have you too, but... well, maybe next time. Right, Kiddo?"

Jason smiled. "Right," he drawled, hanging onto the 'i'.

Andrew frowned slightly and then turned to his daughter. "Almost set, Princess?" He turned back to Jason and added, "We need to go shopping before we leave. She can't go to Chicago like that."

Liz bristled slightly. She was all too aware that awareness of the game between her and Andrew did not end the gut level emotions that he constantly stirred in her.

Jason stood quietly, watching. Just like old times, he thought. Yeah, just like old times.

The phone rang and Jason excused himself to answer it. Thank God for small miracles, he sighed, and lifted the receiver.

"Hello?"

"Jason! It's Andy!"

"Hey, how are you?" he chuckled. She was obviously onto something so he didn't bother to ask. He just waited.

"Can you get out?"

"I don't know. My dad's here."

"Your dad?"

"Yeah. A surprise visit. Isn't that great." Jason glanced over his shoulder toward the kitchen. He could still hear his dad's voice so there was no danger of his dad hearing him.

"We need to go to the library," Andy continued. "I want to research this time displacement thing further."

"How?" Jason asked.

"I don't know, but there has to be something on ghosts, or time according to ghosts, or something like that."

"Ghost time? I don't know, Andy. I think we're getting a little far out there."
"Jason, this is important. It would explain a lot."

"Like what?"
"Well... look, never mind. I'll just go by myself."
"No you won't. I'll meet you at the library in twenty minutes."

As Jason hung up the receiver, he turned to find his dad, arms folded, watching him.

"Can't stick around to talk with your dad?"

"Uh... sorry dad. This is important."

Andrew threw his hands up in the air. "Hey, I'm the intruder here. I understand."

Jason knew what the desired response would be, and he could have done it, but instead he passed by his dad and went into the kitchen to find his mom. Deenie was talking with her mom about which doll clothes should be packed and fell silent at Jason's appearance. Jason crouched next to her and said, "Miss me?"

Deenie nodded, her big eyes moistening. Jason smiled. "You'll have so much fun, you won't even remember to call, I bet."

Deenie pouted, "Oh yes I will!"

"Promise?" Jason asked.

Deenie grinned and standing up abruptly said, "Cross my heart and hope to die!"

Jason embraced her. "You have fun," he said, and then

pressing his lips to her hair, whispered, "If you need me, I'm here."

Liz looked on, the knot in her stomach tightening.

Suddenly, Jason pulled away. "Don't move," he said, and disappeared up the stairs to his room. He was back a few minutes later and crouched at her side again, as though he had never been gone at all.

"Where's your purse?" he asked. "Go get it."

Deenie obliged, excited by the attention and the makings of a game.

"Good." Jason said after she had returned. "Now, I have something for you. I want you to keep it in your purse or with you all the time. If you leave your purse at home, take this out and put it in your pocket. Do you understand?"

Deenie nodded, eyes shining.

"If you ever need me, or are lost and need to come home, use it and someone will help you find me and mom again. Do you understand?"

Eyes ablaze, Deenie nodded vigorously. This was a magic piece. And it was for her!

Jason pulled an old medallion out of his pocket. It was about the size of a silver dollar and was suspended from a chain. Jason had gotten it at a carnival years ago, and each time he had cleaned his room, for some reason he always skipped it over for throwing away. Eventually he had begun to think there was a reason he kept it all these years and so he continued to keep it. Now he knew why.

The medallion was engraved with his name and address on one side and on the other the words, "Please help the bearer find me." Jason placed the piece in Deenie's out-stretched hands and watched her face as she examined it. Then, with as serious a look as a four-year-old can muster, Deenie unzipped her purse and placed the piece in the side pocket. She then re-zipped the purse and looked at her brother. Placing the shoulder strap of the purse over her small shoulder, she then placed her arms around her brother's neck and hugged him. "Don't worry," she whispered. "I'll be back before you know it."

Jason smiled into her hair and gave her a small squeeze.

CHAPTER 9

Andy paced impatiently in front of the library. It had been half an hour and no Jason. Normally the appearance of Jason's dad would have been ripe material for her overactive imagination, but not today. Today the concept of Time was all Andy could think about.

While walking home the night before, she and Scat had discussed at length each other's perceptions of the night's events. The horses, once a source of strife between them, had suddenly become the center of both of their foci. Scat was more than eager to view his ideas and perceptions of what had taken place in the field and around it. That seemed to be the key — what went on in the field versus what went on around it.

Andy ran through the events and perceptions in her mind again. "According to Scat, there was no visible mist or fog. And, Jason and I were alone after we found each other for only about five minutes, which is how long it would take two people to walk down the trail to the lake's edge at the base of the rocks."

Andy scanned the road for Jason and then turned back to her thoughts. No mist, but a veil...

A veil...?

"Hi! Sorry I'm late."

Jason jarred Andy back to reality and she scowled. "Something is missing," she said aloud, half to herself and half to Jason.

Jason shrugged and followed Andy as she turned and pulled open the library door.

Miss Carl, the librarian, raised her head enough to peer over her glasses at the new arrivals. She smiled warmly at Andy. Andy was her most regular patron, always looking up one subject or another.

"Hello, Miss Carl," Andy whispered and continued on her way to the rows of card catalogs. Jason's mind was already wandering and he lagged behind at the displays of historical volumes set up across from the librarian's desk and began to leaf through them.

Most of the historical books on display were volumes of records of Five Star. They were filled with comings and goings, births and deaths, and reproductions of news clippings of major events. To amuse himself, Jason began flipping the pages to see if he could recognize any names. He had only been at it for about five minutes when… there he was. Staring back at him from the page was a gentleman who for all the world could have been Jason!

The photo was dated 1939. The inscription read, "Sir Collin Bastion with Raise the Dead." The photo was of a man with a large black horse. They were standing together in a field, the horse loose with no form of restraint. As Jason scanned the photo he was strangely drawn to the background. Behind them in the distance was a lake!

Jason put the open book down on the counter and hurried to where Andy was still busily looking through titles and descriptions of books.

"No luck?" Jason asked.

"Metaphysics is not Five Star's forte," she replied, still searching.

"Maybe it is," Jason replied. "Come look at this."

Andy looked at him questioningly. Seeing she would get no verbal response, she sighed and followed him.

Andy stared at the photo and then a small smile began to spread across her lips. She scanned the biography and then turned to Jason. "It's him, alright."

"Yeah," Jason said. "But it's also me."

Andy didn't seem to hear him. "This biography says he came from England. I wonder if he went back there, too." And then she scooped up the book and went to Miss Carl's desk. She waited patiently for the older woman to look up and then smiled broadly.

"Miss Carl, maybe you could help me." She placed the book down on the desk and pointed to the photo. "The biography here says this man came from England. He doesn't live here now, does he?"

"Good Lord no!" laughed Miss Carl. "Collin Bastion lived here very briefly and then left just as quickly as he came." Then, looking around to be sure no one was near, she leaned over her desk and in a hushed tone added, "I'm sure you kids have heard the legend of the lake. Well, that's him. He's the man in that legend."

Miss Carl settled back into her chair again and sighed, gazing at the picture. "Such a shame. He was such a handsome man."

Andy waited quietly. Miss Carl shook herself from her thoughts and continued. "He went back to England. The poor man was so distraught."

And as though as an afterthought, she looked at Andy directly and said, "Half of the horses were never found, you know."

Andy glanced at Jason. "I thought they died, Miss Carl?"

"Heavens no!" she laughed. "Some of them did; animals got them they think."

"I thought they had a disease or something."

Miss Carl laughed again. "That's the legend. Convenient, too."

Andy waited again, this time not so patiently. Jason was hanging on every word and decided to chime in. "If the horses weren't the reason, then why did he leave?"

Miss Carl suddenly looked at Jason, as if noticing him there for the first time. She decided that he was okay and finally said, "No one knows. No one knows any of it for sure. Rumor was that he had his heart broken by a gal." And then turning to Andy in a conspiratorial whisper, she continued. "More likely that a gal had her heart broken by him." She turned back to both of them. "That doesn't explain the horses though. All of it is just rumors though; nothing to hang a hat on. No one really knows." And, as an afterthought, she added, "No one ever really will."

"Why do you say that?" asked Andy.

Miss Carl looked at Andy and laughed. "Well, dear, that's just the kind of man Collin Bastion was. No one knew his business back then. It doesn't make any sense to think that anyone will know his business now."

Andy was frowning in thought. Jason stared silently at the photo, and then he realized something – both he and Andy had noticed immediately how similar he looked to this Collin fellow, but Miss Carl had made no reference. Jason looked up to find her staring at him. She blushed, then smiled; her eyes a-glitter.

By the time Jason got home, Deenie and his father were long gone. His mother was stretched out on the couch reading a book. When she heard him come in, she called to him to come join her.

"Deenie get off okay?" he asked.

"Fine," she replied, "and I'm adjusting. I've been thinking, though."

Jason watched her, looking for signs, and saw none.

"You remember our 'boyfriend' conversation?"

Jason laughed. "Yeah?"

"Would you mind if I started having him over on occasion? Deenie will be away for a month or so, and I'd like for you to meet him."

Jason felt his emotions taking over, but he could not quite figure out which one was in the lead. Jealousy, anger, fear, annoyance, sorrow... yet all at once glad, proud, relieved.

Liz continued, when he didn't immediately respond. "I know it's somewhat selfish of me, but I could use the company. I can't expect you to stay around all the time."

Jason realized he had not answered and snapped back to the present. "Fine, Mom. I think it's a great idea. I mean, it'll take some getting used to, but it'll be fine. You deserve it." He watched his mother, a faint smile spreading across her face. Just like old times, he thought. "Hell," he said, "you know what I mean."

Liz laughed.

Jason got up and had started toward the stairs when he suddenly stopped. He turned and looked at his mother. Trying to do some quick math in his head, Jason frowned and then shook his head as if to say he gave up. Then looking again at his mother, he said, "Forget it," aloud and turned and headed for the stairs again. Liz shrugged and returned to her book. "He'll come to me when he's ready," she thought.

CHAPTER 10

"Jason! Liz is on the phone!"

"Liz!" Jason thought to himself. He had forgotten. And now suddenly every detail of her and the night before came rushing back, threatening to dissolve him. He sat down on the edge of the bed breathing in the scent of her hair when his mother appeared at the door.

"Jason, did you hear me? Liz is on the phone."

Jason forced his attention to the present and turned slowly to face his mother. "Sorry, yeah, Mom. I do," he said.

Liz smiled and crossed her arms. "You do what, honey?" she asked.

Jason looked puzzled and she laughed. "Okay," she said, "I'll show you where the phone is."

Jason smiled, shaking his head, "I think I can find the way," he said.

Liz shook her head as Jason brushed past her and headed for the phone.

Jason lifted the receiver to his ear and listened. As the sound of her breathing began to intoxicate him, Liz cut in. "Jason? Are you there?"

"Oh... hi," he stuttered.

Liz was silent, and then, as though she could see through the line, she began again.

"Jason, this is Liz. A lot went on last night and I just wanted to call and say I had a very nice time."

Jason's mind began to clear. Nice time... went on... the lake! Liz was there, too!

Liz continued, "I still don't know what to make of a lot of it, but... well... I like you. And your company."

"Thanks. I mean I did, too. I really enjoyed your company." Jason glanced around and continued. "Would you like to go for a walk?"

Liz was quiet for a moment. "Sure," she replied.

"I mean now. I'd like to see you. Please?"

Liz could feel a smile spreading over her face. "That would be great," she said, trying not to sound as excited as she felt.

"Great," Jason said. "I'll be right over." And he hung up.

His mother was waiting when he came back down the stairs. Clean shirt, clean shorts.

"Will you be out late?" she asked. She somehow knew this was not the time for jokes, and she waited patiently for whatever answer she might get.

"Two hours at the most," Jason answered, and the kitchen door swung shut behind him.

Fifteen minutes later Jason and Liz were walking down the street headed towards the edge of town. No one had been home when Jason arrived at Liz's house so they had both been spared any awkward, innocent questions Ed or Marla may have asked them. Liz had met Jason on the porch at 6:30 PM. It was not like Ed and Marla not to be home at this hour, but Liz didn't question it. The note had said "Gone for air – back in an hour," and the time of 6:00 PM had been printed at the top. "It's good for them to get out," Liz thought, and she couldn't help but think that somehow she and Jason had played a part. All day Ed and Marla sat on the porch, chatting easily with passers-by. Ed had even gone to the gate on a few occasions to shake hands with new neighbors or, at Marla's behest, to invite tired faces up to the porch for a cool drink. Liz had watched with amusement, but deep inside she was glad. Ed and Marla were such sweet folks; she hated to see them alone all the time. So, whatever the reason, it was fine with her. Everywhere, all around, things were changing.

Jason and Liz walked in silence until they reached the edge of town. As they passed the last street of houses, the road stretched on forever into nowhere, or so it seemed. As far as they could see, it reached for the horizon until it faded into the haze. Jason led them on for another two minutes and then took a dirt path that led off to the left of the main road. In the distance Liz could see some rocks jutting out of what had seemed to be immutable flatness.

She had never been this far out of town before and she began to wonder where Jason was taking her.

"Are we going somewhere special?" she asked.

Jason turned to her and smiled. "Someplace quiet," he said. He turned to look at the rocks ahead and continued. "I used to come here a lot when my family first moved here. It's very quiet and it's a great place to sit and think."

Liz was puzzled and Jason could sense it, so he rambled on, fishing for something that would make more sense to her while still retaining the transience of his feelings.

"Actually, I've never brought anyone up here before. This was sort of on an impulse. You may hate it, but it's special to me. I just thought I'd show it to you and then you could see a side of me that people don't usually see."

Liz smiled and feigned an even more puzzled look. "I thought we weren't going anywhere special?" she teased.

Jason stopped. They had reached the foot of the rocks and it was time to decide whether or not they went on or turned back.

"When my family first moved here, things were not happy at my house," Jason explained. "I used to come here to get away from the noise. To find quiet. Jason slid his hand over the smooth rocks that signaled the start of the path, thinking of his next words carefully.

It's quiet here, but it's not lonely quiet. Well... actually, it can be. The rocks here, they give you what you want. They reflect your soul back for you to see. So, pretty soon I figured out that when I had a problem, I could come here to see more clearly what it was that was bothering me. I would sort of just... know what to do. Does that make sense?"

Jason waited patiently for Liz to digest what he had just said. When she finally spoke, he was relieved.

"So, what you're saying is that you come here to clear your head and reflect on what's going on inside you rather than always focusing on yourself in terms of what is going on outside you."

Being with someone that understood him so easily, so

naturally, would take some getting used to. Jason took Liz's hand. "Let's climb," he said.

Jason turned and led the way up a narrow path that wound its way through and up into the outcropping of rocks. Liz was vaguely aware that she hadn't noticed any trail being there before, but she dismissed it. The path was narrow and, despite Jason obviously slowing his pace for her, she needed to give her feet all her attention. Most of the trail lay wedged between steep rocks that rose ever higher on both sides of them, giving the illusion that they traveled downward rather than up. Yet when they emerged into a clearing, the panorama before them affirmed that they were indeed high among the foothills.

"It's beautiful," Liz whispered. A sudden breeze seemed to lift the words from her lips and send them to Jason, who turned to her and smiled. He stretched out his hand toward her and, when she took it, led her toward the edge of the plateau. Liz began to hesitate as they neared the edge, and Jason reassured her, "It's okay. It's not steep." Liz took the final steps and peered over the edge. To her surprise, what had seemed to be a cliff was actually a short six-foot slope to the plateau below. Jason frowned slightly as images of galloping horses flitted across his mind. He looked toward the plateau below and the small cluster of plants that grew at the base of the rock wall. They were some of the only plants that he had ever found up here. A small spring of water gurgled up into a self-made pool at the base of the rocks. From deep inside the rocks the water came, no doubt released by some ancient shifting, freeing the water here only until another shifting collapsed its route and sent the water somewhere else. Jason contemplated the spring as he always did, aware that there was more there than he was seeing, but not quite sure what.

Jason became very aware of Liz's presence, as though she had suddenly arrived. When he glanced at her, she too was watching the water. When she became aware of Jason focusing on her, she spoke softly. "Do you ever feel like the spring is talking to you, but that you can't quite understand the words?"

Jason's eyes widened in surprise. "That's it!" he thought. "That's the feeling!"

Unaware of his reaction, Liz continued. "Can we get closer? Maybe I can tell better if I am closer."

Jason looked toward the sky. The sun was bright red in the distance as it covered the last few inches of sky before melting into the horizon.

"It's getting late," Jason said, "and we still need to get you back down that trail."

Liz sighed and nodded slowly, still watching the water.

"We can come back," Jason added, although he was not actually sure when that would be. This place was funny like that. You didn't really plan to come here; you just sort of ended up here, like you had been summoned or something. You never realize it, though, until you actually get here.

The night settled down around everything in earnest just as Jason and Liz reached the end of the dirt path and turned onto the main road headed back toward town. Being on paved road once again appeared to have some sort of ritualistic effect for both of them, for they both began to take notice of their surroundings as though they had just returned from a distant place. In fact, this was not far from the truth. Both had been so absorbed in thought that neither had noticed even the passing of the scenery. Jason's steps were purely instinctual. He had passed this way so often before he no longer needed to direct his feet. They knew the way on their own.

It was then that he became aware that the only thing keeping Liz with him on the journey back was his delicate grasp on her fingers. He suddenly became very conscious of the index and middle finger of her left hand firmly pressed into the palm of his right hand. Not a very secure link, he mused to himself. And then it struck him – would he have noticed had her fingers slipped away? Would he have noticed if she no longer followed?

Jason turned his head slightly to glance at her out of the corner of his eye. Liz was frowning slightly in thought, but she too had forced herself to focus her mind's wanderings enough to include some attention to her immediate surroundings. As she felt Jason's glance, she returned it with a smile.

Jason sighed, shifting his hold on her hand to encompass the whole thing. Liz accepted this sign of affection from him by lifting his hand to her shoulder and snuggling up under his arm, her hand finally coming to rest on his hip holding him to her. As Jason passed his arm around her shoulder, Liz tilted her head slightly so it lay against his chest.

Jason suddenly became very aware that if he just turned his face slightly toward her, her cheek would be only inches from his lips. Her soft, silky cheek. He recalled suddenly the night before at the dance. The memory of the taste of her tantalized him. Jason allowed himself to be caught between that memory and the awareness of her nearness and let the waves from it wash over him. It was a sort of tingling sensation that started low in his belly, welling up from deep inside him and then spreading out in waves, reaching all parts and points of his body and leaving him both invigorated and depleted.

The pace of their walking slowed so that any passers-by would think they're just out for an evening stroll. Liz tilted her face upward so that she was looking up into Jason's face. Instinctively, she always seemed to know when a moment was right, as she did now. Jason looked into her face – her half-closed blue eyes dancing with the fire of her soul, and her lips pouting slightly, even when she smiled. And now, slightly parted in her smile, they beckoned him.

Jason was not aware that he was kissing her, or going to kiss her, until he felt the moistness of her lips against his. He had brushed them gently, lingering for perhaps a second too long, reluctant to end the feel of her lips against his. And then, without warning, he felt the swell. The wave came, rising up, surging through his veins. And as it reached its peak, threatening to explode him, he stopped his forward motion, pulling Liz into his arms and tight against him, all in one liquid motion.

With her face still tilted upward, Jason closed his mouth down hard against hers. The part in her lips beckoned him. The feel of her body pressed against his only exacerbated the tension in his groin, and he gingerly explored the space between her lips with his tongue. With one arm firmly across her shoulders and the other pressing her pelvis to his, Jason tightened his hold and kissed her harder. Her tongue found his, caressing him, inviting him. Jason ran his hand over her buttocks, feeling their firmness, acutely aware of the firmness of her breasts pressed against his chest.

"I'm sorry," he said, releasing his hold and stepping back. "I don't know what's come over me. I'm being very rude. I'm… I'm sorry." His eyes looked toward the ground. He was confused by his own intentions and yet intrigued by his own actions. At fifteen, he had not yet had a real girlfriend to speak of. Maybe girls who he had stolen kisses from behind the bleachers in the schoolyard, but never anything like this.

"Showing affection for someone isn't rude," Liz said quietly.

Jason looked up, startled. His eyes met hers and he could feel the tension rising again.

"It's not very gentleman-like," he replied.

Liz laughed. "Even gentlemen have to express their desires, especially if it involves someone they are attracted to." She paused, her eyes locked on Jason's. "Are you attracted to me, Jason?" she whispered, feigning innocence.

It took a split second for Jason to cover the space between them. He took her face in both of his hands and, unhesitatingly pressed his lips to hers, his tongue eagerly seeking hers. Liz encircled his waist with her arms and, leaning her pelvis against his, began to caress his back.

Jason thought he had ended up in heaven. He drew his lips from Liz's and, enfolding her in his arms, pressed her face to his shoulder and began caressing her hair. They held each other like that for some time and, when their senses finally cleared, realized that others would be worrying and that they should be pressing on.

It was nine-thirty when Liz and Jason arrived at her house. No one was about, so Jason walked her to the porch and kissed her chastely. Liz smiled at the effort, a longing playing at the corners of her mouth. Jason stroked her cheek and returned the message, a longing evident in his smile as well.

"I still owe Marla berries," Jason said, matter-of-factly.

"I'd love to join your berry picking," Liz intoned, the lilt in her voice amplifying her humor.

Jason laughed and she joined him. "I'll call you in the morning," he added, and brushing her lips with his one last time, he took the porch steps two at a time and began his walk home.

Jason's mom looked at the clock for the fourth time in the last half hour. It was nine-thirty and Jason still wasn't home yet. It wasn't like her son to be late without letting her know. That and the constant unanswered ringing at Andrew's house were bringing her close to the edge. She had called six times and each time she had gotten nothing but a monotone ringing. Andrew had said he would call when they got in. Liz sighed. She had believed him. Since when did Andrew do anything that didn't suit himself? The nagging at the back of her mind persisted, though, and she forced herself to push it away. "Now where is Jason?" she thought.

She heard the back door open but for some reason this didn't comfort her. As Jason came into the kitchen, Liz suddenly felt out of place. What was she dong there? She cast a furtive glance at Jason and whispered hello.

Jason looked at her. "Mom, are you okay?"

The tear slid down Liz's cheek, charting its own lazy path down the slope of her face. And now it was Jason's turn to feel out of place.

"Fine," Liz muttered, and turned to leave, heading for the sanctuary of her room. Jason looked after her, confused. Somehow he knew this had nothing to do with him, yet somehow it probably included him too. He shrugged off the guilt that was rising up in him and looked at the kitchen clock. Ten o'clock. It had been a long day. And for the first time, his mind drifted to thoughts of his sister and he hoped she was having fun.

CHAPTER 11

Jason woke with a start. Sitting up, he felt a cold, clammy sweat hug his body as he strained to hear the noise. He had dreamt of screaming horses, their guttural cries echoing loudly still. It had seemed so real, as though he could hear them through his sleep, not just in it.

There! There it was again! Muffled, yes, but most definitely. Only he was awake, not dreaming, and the realization woke him for good. He jumped out of bed and on quick, silent feet was out his bedroom door and down the stairs. He came to rest before the front door. Halted in his mission, he took a deep breath and slowly reached for the lock. Sliding back the bolt, he turned the knob and pulled the front door open, shutting his eyes tight as he did so. With the door open, he slowly opened his eyes, wider and wider.

"Oh my God," he whispered. He stepped out onto the front porch and silently pulled the door closed behind him. There, milling in the yard, were the horses.

A light suddenly illuminated the ground to the left of the porch. "Damn," he said aloud. His mother had woken and no doubt was coming to see what all the noise was about. And how exactly would he explain this? He walked off the porch, arms extended, waving them at the milling animals. They seemed to pay no attention to his wild gestures, although he was aware that all the while they were focused on him, waiting. He looked behind him at the door. Time was short. "Shoo," he hissed. A sense of urgency was devouring him and he waved his arms all the more.

He suddenly became aware of a young, soft gray horse directly before him. It had stopped to stare, and now it tossed its head in seeming indignation. Jason looked at the animal, suddenly fixated on the details of it. He could almost see through it!

The horse had very delicate features, from the long, slender face to the fine bone structure of its body. This was accented by a long, silky mane and tail set against a soft, gray body. Every detail of the young animal's body was acutely clear, yet at the same time Jason could see the drifting forms and details of the other horses behind it, through its body.

The young horse tossed its head again. Jason took a step toward it and, without even realizing what he was doing, reached out his hand toward the soft, delicate nose.

The door swung open and the young horse threw its head up with a start. Rising majestically on its hind legs, it spun about and Jason lost it in the herd. Looking behind him he saw his mother. Her face ashen white, she stood on the porch, her hands at her mouth to stifle the scream.

Jason was at her side in an instant. "It's okay, Mom."

Somehow even he knew how ineffectual that sounded. Liz looked at him with wild eyes.

"It's okay, mom." She repeated the words slowly, giving the effect of pouring syrup. Jason squeezed her arm and her eyes dropped to where he was touching her. Jason turned to the herd. They were packed tighter now, uneasy at the sight of Liz, yet reluctant to leave. Jason released his hold on Liz's arm and stepped to the edge of the porch. Shutting his eyes in concentration, he finally opened them and with a wave of his arm released the animals.

"To the lake!" His voice rang clear, and then they were gone.

Liz's eyes opened wide in surprise. She gingerly advanced until she was standing at his side. She peered into the yard, careful to look into all the corners. For some reason the darkness made no difference in this endeavor. Her instincts told her that there was nothing out there.

Sitting together in the living room, neither said a word. Liz stared into the darkness. Neither had the desire to light the room when they came in, so they sat with the darkness as a security blanket. Neither had anything to say, yet they both knew something needed to be said.

Jason examined his hands in the gloom. The moonlight filtering in gave the room a Cimmerian atmosphere and although the room was not that dark, even after he had become accustomed to the dimness he was still unable to make out the details of his fingers. As a result, his mind drifted back to the details of the young horse.

He had not noticed at the lake that the horses were not solid. It fascinated him, the anomalous aura that surrounded them, and him, when they were around. He remembered the time at the lake when he and Andy had watched them running in the distance, and how odd he had felt afterward. Both of them had stared into the trees long after the creatures had disappeared, looking for a sign that they had not merely been specters of the wind and rain, formed from their imaginations out of the intensities of their desires. How long ago that night seemed.

Liz's mind gradually began to slow. Time seemed to be racing with her, and she was convinced that she was slowly but surely losing ground. She didn't know what to make of what had just happened, yet she couldn't get the image of her young daughter out of her mind. It seemed ludicrous to her -- she had found her son in their front yard in the middle of the night with a herd of horses and all she could think of was the fact that there was no answer at Andrew's house.

"I don't understand why he doesn't answer the phone," she said, still staring into the safety of the air.

Jason didn't answer. He hadn't heard. He was reaching, fingers extended, for the soft velvety nose of a small, gray horse that was stretching its nose toward him.

CHAPTER 12

Andrew Coussens caught himself sighing for the tenth time that morning. He had shown them. The first thing he had done when he had arrived home yesterday was to turn off his answering machine. So what if other people couldn't reach him; the ones who counted knew his cell phone number and that didn't include his ex-wife. Deenie had asked why he didn't answer his phone, and he had told her that it was probably just telemarketers. Not knowing what such a person was, Deenie inquired, and then scolded her father for not allowing those people to at least attempt to sell him something by answering the phone. This had prompted his sighing. Like father like daughter.

Sure, sure, he could have just unplugged the phone, but that would ruin the game since then he wouldn't know how often Liz had tried to call. It was just for today anyway; he would call tomorrow. Deenie would insist on it. Every time the phone rang it reminded her that she needed to call her mother and it was becoming increasingly difficult to distract her from that thought.

When the phone rang for the third time, Andrew gave up and herded his daughter to the community pool to get her out of earshot of the phone. Jessica, his girlfriend, had been none too happy about the surprise switch in children, but she was a trooper.

The promise of a trip to the jewelry store guaranteed it.

The phone rang again. Andrew smiled. "Number four," he said aloud to the empty room.

"Okay honey, you can go in the pool, but don't drown or anything. This suit isn't supposed to get wet. It's just for sunning."

Deenie rolled her eyes. "I'll try my best," she said, and made her way over to the stairs.

The pool wasn't too crowded. Jessica had taken over the area at the shallow end of the pool. She didn't like to be splashed or crowded and this kept the risk down. There weren't any kids living in this complex so the occasional few that visited never presented much of a problem. Along the long sides of the pool were some scattered residents. The Red Hat Ladies, as she liked to call them, were clustered around a table shaded by a parasol, playing cards as usual, and two older gentlemen had positioned themselves in their usual spot in direct view of Jessica. It was their daily prayer that when she flipped over she might come out of her top, if even for a moment. At their age, it would be worth it.

Jessica knew the drill, and she rarely disappointed them. They were harmless, those two, and she liked to please. One never knew what the future held or where it would bring you, so she liked to keep all her options open. Right now, her current option was becoming trying. Sure, Andrew was generous, but she always felt like she was being bought. It wasn't supposed to work that way. Being bought wasn't the problem. Feeling like it was, and that was something she was coming to resent. The small girl making her way down the stairs of the pool only served to fuel her resentment, and so brought a frown to her face. "Not good," she whispered to herself, running her fingers over the creases of her frowning forehead. "Not good at all." Maybe she would skip the trip to the jewelry store and trade it for a Botox treatment. Andrew wouldn't care.

Deenie made her way down the stairs carefully, one step at a time, her hand on the railing as Jason had showed her. "Most people drown in shallow water, not the deep end," Jason had cautioned her, "so take care no matter how deep the water." She took whatever Jason said to heart. He never steered her wrong, and she had no intention of letting him down by drowning in shallow water because she hadn't heeded his caution.

Standing solidly on the bottom stair, Deenie watched the pool bottom fan out before her. She had watched a few people enter and exit the water so she had an idea of the depth, and this was as far as she was going. She wished Jason were here. He would rescue her... he would come for her through the water, her trusty dolphin steed, and rescue her from the dreaded land people who held her captive here on the stairs. Then she, the mermaid princess, would ride him off to the magic mermaid city...

"Excuse me," came an old voice, and Deenie turned to see a frail elderly woman slowly navigating the pool steps, much like she had just done, and using the rail as her crutch.

In a serious voice, Deenie replied, "I'm sorry, ma'am, but I can't let go of the railing. If I let go before my dolphin steed arrives, I'll get swept out to the depths and drown."

The woman raised an eyebrow, and then, as best she could, leaned in towards the small girl, "I know what you mean. The depths of the pool can be treacherous. That's why I hold tight to the railing."

Now it was Deenie's turn to raise an eyebrow, and then the two broke into smiles together. "How about if I go up a step, and then you can come down a step," said Deenie, and then ever so carefully the two passed, until Deenie was on the step above and the elder woman on the step below.

"I'm Miranda," said the woman, and Deenie replied in kind.

"Nice to meet you, Deenie," Miranda continued. "It is so hard to find other princesses to converse with. Do you find that too?"

"Yes, yes I do," said Deenie, casting a glance at Jessica's dozing form.

*　*　*

"Where's Deenie, Sleeping Beauty?" asked Andrew. He scanned the pool area, not so much concerned as irritated. It was a simple task - watch one four year old in a fenced in pool area. He asked again, this time shaking her roughly. "Hey, Sleeping Beauty, where's Deenie?" He should have known it would have been too much to ask. He didn't date Jessica for her brains, nor did she date him for his personality. So they were even.

"Huh, what?" sputtered Jessica. The two older gentlemen leaned slightly forward in their seats.

"My daughter; have you seen her?" asked Andrew in an increasingly patronizing tone. It was a familiar one and Jessica ignored it.

"Sure, babe, she's over there," she replied, waving her hand in the general direction of the pool.

Andrew turned his head and met the eyes of the two older gentlemen. Jessica was still in her suit, but they hadn't given up hope. "Jesus Christ," he hissed. He grabbed her cover up and tossed it at her. Jessica smirked as the cotton shift slapped her in the chest.

"I've lived here quite some time, dear," answered Miranda. "It's a nice place, but alas, no princesses. You are the first. How long will you be here?"

"Until it's time to go home," replied Deenie, eyeing the cookies that Miranda had put out for them. She had never had lemonade with cookies. Her mother usually served milk, but that was okay. Miranda was a real princess so maybe this was how princesses did it. She had a lot to learn.

"Would you like a cookie, Dear?" queried Miranda, offering the plate. Deenie was fascinated by the plate, and strategically removed a cookie so as to see more of the pattern. It was a small, flat disk of white China, rimmed in a relief pattern. Among the lazy vines making their way around the plate cavorted small horses.

Miranda noticed the girl's attention and smiled. "It's a pretty plate, isn't it?"

"Yes," replied Deenie, squinting to see the horses better.

"I found it at a rummage sale," continued Miranda. "It seemed so out of place there, so I purchased it and brought it home. It seems much happier here."

A rapid knocking broke the plate's spell and Miranda gave Deenie a knowing look, masked with a cheery, "Now who could that be?"

Deenie sighed. She had a good idea. "It's the land people. They've come to take me back."

Miranda cocked an eyebrow, "Oh dear. Well, I guess we don't have much time then." Miranda reached over and patted Deenie's hand. "You are always welcome here. Always." Deenie smiled her thanks.

Miranda made her way to the door and called, "Who is it?"

"Andrew Coussens," came the terse answer.

Miranda looked over her shoulder at Deenie and shrugged her shoulders. Deenie nodded. Miranda opened the door and the land people entered.

"Deenie," Andrew said, although it sounded more like a command than a statement of fact. "We were worried sick. You shouldn't go off like that." And turning to Miranda, he added, "And you should know better than to leave with someone's child without permission."

Miranda looked at Andrew with her best blank face, smiling with a vacuous sweetness that belied the actual clarity of her mind. Frail she might be, but her mind was still sharp. She had enjoyed the young girl immensely and appreciated her vivid imagination, although at this point she was beginning to wonder if the concept of "land people" might not be a valid one.

"Come on, Deenie, time to go," Andrew commanded. Deenie slid slowly from her chair and walked toward her father. Suddenly, she brightened, and asked, "When are we calling Mom?"

CHAPTER 13

The ringing of the phone woke Jason at 7:15 AM. Liz had it before the second ring, but Jason's sleep had been troubled as it was. The phone signaled that morning was here, meaning that the interruptions would only increase in number.

The strained cheer in his mother's voice told him it was his father calling, finally. He did recall that much of their conversation in the dark last night. He hadn't attempted to placate her. There was nothing to say. Deenie was fine, of that they were both sure, but his father was toying with his mother again. Jason's anger rose with the early morning light.

Liz knocked lightly and cracked the door. "That was your father. It sounds like Deenie is running him ragged already." Jason smiled, hoping it was the correct response. The phone rang again and Liz disappeared again. Jason took the opportunity to rouse himself for good.

"Jason, it's for you," his mom called. It had to be Andy. Who else could be up and on the go at this hour?

Jason took the phone and said hello as alertly as he could.

"Meet me in front of the library in an hour."

"Andy? Good morning to you too."

"It's important."

"Okay. Not a problem."

He sensed a hang up was coming and was pleasantly surprised when it didn't happen.

"How are you, Jason?" Andy asked tentatively.

"I'm fine," he replied, which was true. Oddly enough, he was just fine.

Jason checked the clock in the library. It was almost eight-thirty and Andy was late. Andy was never late. She took pride in being the first one to arrive no matter where she went. Jason went in to Miss Carl's desk to see if she had seen Andy, but Miss Carl was nowhere to be found either. The library felt oddly quiet today. Not that it was ever loud, but this was an eerie quiet, a total lack of noise. And warmth. For a warm July day, it was cool; too cool.

Jason whispered loudly into the cool air, "Miss Carl? Andy?" No response, only a faint rustling in the stacks to the rear of the library. Jason headed for it.

The library was small, and the central corridor extended from the ornate double wooden front doors straight to the back. Miss Carl's desk, which was actually four desks arranged in a square, sat in the center of the corridor, so that anyone who entered or left fell under her watchful eye. Along the corridor, stacks extended to the right and left, and at the rear of the building the space fanned out to accommodate several wing chairs arranged around an old defunct fireplace. A round table with six or so mismatched chairs sat in the corner.

Jason slowed as he reached the end of the corridor, scanning the area before him for the source of the rustling. Seated in one of the wing chairs with his back to the corridor was a lone gentleman. He casually turned the pages of a large book and appeared to be enjoying the glow of the fire in the fireplace. Jason turned to go back the way he came, but frowned and turned back to the man. Although the fireplace was stone cold, the glow of a warming blaze played around the gentleman's head like a halo. Jason took a step closer. Without a glance in his direction, the gentleman casually waved to the chair to his left, a seemingly general invitation for whomever was approaching to join him. Jason accepted and moved slowly around the far side of the chair, eyes fixed on the top of the man's head in the hopes that a slight movement would unveil the identity of his new host. Jason lowered himself slowly into the chair. The gentleman continued to peruse the large book before him.

"The whispers of the walls have basis," said the man casually.

Andy's voice drifted back to the rear of the building. Jason couldn't make out the words, but the gentleman cocked his head slightly, apparently improving his own reception. As the voices began to grow louder, the shadows around the gentleman's face smiled wearily. He gathered himself to rise, his face finally emerging from the book. He gazed directly into Jason's eyes as he rose and, placing the book on the chair, stepped toward the fireplace and vanished.

Jason watched, oddly unfazed. He reached over and hefted the book onto his own lap. He didn't have to read the cover to know what it was; he had looked at this very same book the last time he was here. A slip of paper was neatly tucked into it and Jason turned to the page it marked. Jason looked at the photo. He didn't need to read the inscription. He knew the photo, and he mouthed, "Sir Collin Bastion with Raise the Dead."

"Jason, here you are. What are you doing back here?"

It was Andy's voice. Beside her was Scat.

"Enjoying the…" Jason glanced at the cold grate and decided maybe another subject would be better. "Where have you been? It's not like you to be…" Strike two. As he glanced at the clock on the wall he had the strangest sensation.

"I was going to ask the same thing of you. We've been out front since eight o'clock. How did you get in here anyway?" Andy had been looking around the room since she arrived, as though looking for something she knew was there, but not wanting to seem too obvious about it.

Jason looked back at the book on his lap and his attention went to the paper that had been tucked into its pages. He unfolded it to find familiar writing, and read: "Have breakfast with me? My house, 9 AM today. – Liz" He glanced at the clock again, and without even a glance in their direction, said "I have to go," and headed for the door.

"Jason!" cried Andy, and she set off after him.

Scat watched Andy go. This ghost hunting business was unfamiliar turf for him and it was always best to get the lay of the land before butting in, so he let her go. If she didn't return soon he would just head home. He glanced over at the book Jason had put aside, picked it up and began to flip through it to pass the time. It opened on its own to a portrait of a striking blonde woman, standing in a field. Behind her and to the left was a large black horse. Behind the horse in the distance were more horses grazing at the edge of a large lake. The description read, "Unknown Woman, 1938." Scat furrowed his brows. The woman looked familiar somehow. He flipped to the next page and his eyes grew wide as he scanned a second photo. He flipped back and forth between the two photos a few times. He did know that woman. She looked exactly like Jason's mother! He settled into a chair to see what else the book had to offer.

Andy returned a short time later to find Scat deep in thought with what appeared to be a large book. Scat eagerly showed Andy what he had discovered. When Andy saw the photo of the woman, and began to press him for more details.

"So you don't think this woman is 'unknown' after all?" Andy began.

"It would seem unlikely," said Scat. "She's posed in what appears to be the same field as Sir Colin Bastion, the man on the following page. Where they are posed has a very distinctive look, and the horses they are posed with don't look like average, every day horses either." Andy nodded in agreement, taking it all in. It was nice to have someone else doing some of the research for a change.

"I'm no expert on horses," Scat continued, "but those are nice looking ones."

"Do you think it's possible that it's a staged picture?" asked Andy. "You know, a backdrop or something?"

Scat squinted at the photos again, and then asked Andy to see if she could scrounge up a magnifying glass. She returned in a flash sporting a large round one and handed it to Scat. He examined the photos again, and finally said, "No chance. The black horse is in a different position in each and the horses in the background are definitely different. I'd say these were two individual photographs posed at the same location, but at different times." Andy perused the photos with him through the glass and, feeling that this base was covered, moved on to her next question.

"And the man and the woman?" Andy queried. She had been saving this part of the conversation for last.

"Beats me," said Scat. "I guess maybe there really is two of everyone in the world; it's just weird that they'd be in the same family."

"Same family?" Andy asked. "Why do you say that?" Scat grinned. "You're going to love this," he said, and went through the history he had uncovered about the man and the woman with her, slowly.

* * *

Promptly at 9 AM, a man stepped out of the air at the foot of the driveway of the Jason's house. To the casual passer-by it would seem that he had been there all along and they had just not noticed him until now. He glided to the front door in one fluid motion and rang the bell. Jason's mother, Liz, glanced at the clock and smiled – 9 AM on the dot.

Liz opened the front door and smiled. "I see you got my note?"

"I always do," he replied, which was true. No matter where he was, the notes always seemed to find him.

He had first noticed her at the library. He had been vulnerable then; longing for the old days of romance and courtship, and so he had gone to the library to peruse the old books, the old photos. She had been there that day, and so familiar. He resisted for a time, but then told himself, what was the harm? It could not last, that he knew. It would just be a short term amusement until things got better at home. And now he was at her home.

This was the first time the notes had led him to her home. In the past, their meetings had always led to casual encounters – a cup of coffee at 6 AM, an ice cream at midnight, a walk in the park at dusk. Her manner would never have belied her penchant for off hours, but it suited him fine so he didn't question it. He did once explore whether he was somehow encouraging the odd times and places of the meetings, but no, the notes had begun on their own. He had merely followed their trail.

The first note he had found at the library. Sitting by the fire, perusing the book, he found it tucked between the pages. On a card smelling of lavender, he had read, "Meet me tonight. I'll be waiting in my dreams. – Liz."

How he had known where to find her, he could not tell, but he found her in that space of wonder between waking and death, the place we call dreams. The magic of that night had never left him, and yet now he felt uneasy. Did she know, really know, who he was, or the role he was casting her in? Was this meeting going too far?

He pushed his misgivings aside and followed Liz to the rear of the house where she had breakfast set up on the picnic table.

"Delightful," he murmured, and glancing back at her, he was caught by her eyes. Without thinking, he reached for her hand. "Do you mind?" he implored.

Liz blushed. "Of course not," and before he had a chance to rethink his decision, she entwined her fingers in his.

Liz gasped and shook her head, trying to clear it. Suddenly, they were standing in a field; horses grazed in the distance and beyond them was a large lake. Liz shook her head again, but nothing changed. She dropped her eyes, noticing for the first time the long cream-colored dress that had replaced the outfit she had so carefully chosen this morning. She turned to her breakfast-mate and saw that his clothes too had changed.

Her eyes asked the question that her lips could not form, and he took her arm and steered her toward the picnic table and a seat.

"Lizette, you do not look well suddenly. Please, sit down, I am sure you will feel better in a moment."

The name reached her through her fog. She seemed so far away suddenly, like she was watching herself in a dream. Lizette? She furrowed her brow. No, that wasn't her name. Her name was… Elizabeth…?

"Lizette? Do come sit down, dear."

She looked up at him. Those eyes… mesmerizing… "Of course, Collin dear." She let him guide her to a seat.

CHAPTER 14

Jason slowed as he approached his house, a sense of wariness growing in him. He let himself in through the front door and stopped to listen in the entrance hall. He usually entered through the back door – a holdover from younger days when he had a penchant for going places where his shoes got dirty – but decided that if breakfast were in the kitchen he would rather not walk in on it quite so abruptly. He wasn't sure what exactly to expect, but his instincts told him to stay on guard. Wariness was not new to Jason. It had been a constant companion when his father had lived with them. He was grateful for it now. Silence greeted him. "Mom?" he called out. The only reply was the hum of the refrigerator. Jason walked slowly toward the kitchen, listening.

The kitchen was empty, but the signs of a breakfast were there. Jason looked out towards the backyard. It was a beautiful morning and it would be just like his mother to take advantage of it. He went out onto the back porch and looked out over the yard. Empty as well. Jason turned to go back into the house and a frown wrinkled his brow. Something wasn't quite right. He turned back to the neatly kept backyard and let it sink in. What was it? He couldn't quite put his finger on it, but there was something...

He sat down on the top step of the porch and scanned the

yard for a clue. Nothing. "This is pointless," he murmured to himself, and glanced down, his eyes coming to rest on the remnants of green goop on the flagstone steps. He smiled, recalling his sister and the aloe cat bath. He looked toward the picnic table; Spike's favorite sunbathing spot. No Spike. And much to Jason's surprise, there was no picnic table either! He was up in a flash, looking wildly around. He walked out into the yard and began calling his mother. As he passed over the spot where the picnic table had been, he found her.

Liz could hear him faintly calling her. She tore her eyes from Collin and listened. It was Jason. She sensed an urgency in his calling and her mind snapped to it, listening for the unsaid message the tone and inflection would bring her. Collin watched and smiled. It was easy, much too easy. A moment later the boy stepped into his world.

"Jason!" Liz exclaimed. "Is everything all right?" She stood and went to him.

Jason knew *where* he was, but couldn't quite place *when* this was supposed to be. The lake, the horses, the man; they weren't from today, so when were they from?

"Welcome, Jason," Collin said, his voice belying more enthusiasm than he wished to portray.

Jason had no idea how to address the man, so he said nothing.

"Jason, this is Collin," Liz interjected. "Remember, we had talked about a gentleman I wanted you to meet?"

Jason's insides clenched.

"Jason," Collin added, "why don't you join us for

breakfast?" His manner was casual, but there was a tension there that Jason could not quite put his finger on.

Jason took in the scene before him — their picnic table was now located at the lake, where living, breathing horses grazed at the water's edge; where his mother was dressed in something from the turn of the century; and, to top it all off, where he had arrived at their picnic breakfast by walking through the spot their picnic table had been in his backyard. He took a step back.

"How do you do it?" Jason asked.

Collin raised an eyebrow.

"You know, move things through time."

"I'm afraid I don't understand," Collin replied, a calm look on his face.

"The picnic table, us; how did we get here?"

"You wanted to be here, so you are here," he replied.

"Wanted to be here? I don't know where here is, so how could I want to be here?" replied Jason, his voice taking on an edge.

"But of course you did," Collin replied. "You were looking for us, were you not?"

Jason had no reply for him.

"Your mother heard you calling, and so she opened the way. You merely followed her path."

"And my mother," Jason asked.

"I brought her here."

"Did I ask to be brought here?" asked Liz, suddenly interested. Both men looked at her.

After a pause, Collin replied, "In a manner of speaking, yes. More simply, you wanted to remember."

As if on cue, a large black horse snorted, walked a few paces, and set to grazing again. Jason looked toward the noise and whispered, "Raise the Dead…"

"Yes," replied Collin. "Very good. He is an exceptional animal, perfect in every way. Conformation, size, temperament… and he passes on those traits readily. I have high hopes for his offspring."

Jason scanned the field until he found the colt he was looking for. "And that one?" Jason pointed at a soft gray colt grazing slightly apart from the others. As if on cue, it raised its head, looked the picnickers over and tossed its head as if indignant at the inquiry. Collin smiled. "That, Jason, is you."

The phone began to ring. After four rings, the answering machine picked up and began its cheery monologue. "Hello! If you are looking for Liz or Jason or Deenie, please leave a message!" Beep.

"No answer," Andy stated, turning to Scat for advice.

"Why don't we just go over there?"

"There's no one home."

"Well, maybe they'll be home by the time we get there."

Andy frowned, but shrugged and added, "Your lead," as she hung up the phone. Neither of them knew what to do with what they had found at the library, but both agreed that it would be good to see Jason and his mother again.

Fifteen minutes later they were turning into Jason's street.

Neither had said a word on the trip and the silence continued as they neared the house. Half way down the street Scat took hold of Andy's hand and gave it a squeeze. Andy looked at him, and Scat shrugged. "For luck."

"It looks empty," Andy said. Scat had to agree; Jason's house did look empty. "Let's at least knock," he said. Andy moved toward the front door and got ready to knock, but stopped herself. Scat held his breath. Andy turned to him and said, "Something isn't right. I can feel it." And she turned on her heels and headed around the back.

Scat followed after her, looking over his shoulder as he went. He never could get used to how country folks went in and around one another's yards at will. Where he was from, people got shot for less. Andy's actions made him nervous, and he scanned the street to see who was noticing their movements. No one, as usual. Five Star wasn't called a sleepy little town for nothing.

Andy went up the back steps and tried the door. Before Scat could vocalize his protest, she pushed the door open and went in. Scat stopped at the door as though it had an invisible barrier meant for him and him alone. Andy disappeared into the house and Scat turned and looked out over the yard. He had been to Jason's house a couple of times, but never with the time or inclination to actually see it. The yard was tidy and well cared for, which was no surprise. He walked to the edge of the steps and noticed a small bald spot, the comings and goings of diners' feet having worn the grass where a picnic table must have once stood.

Scat cocked his head. It was faint, but he could have sworn he had heard it. Voices in the air. Familiar voices. Jason's voice. Scat looked over his shoulder and called out. "Andy!"

She appeared at his side almost instantly. "What…"

"Shhhhh!" he cut her off. "Listen," he whispered.

She cocked her head, turning her ear to the yard, and her eyes grew wide. "I hear it," she whispered, "but where is he?"

Jason continued to look at the colt. Neither he nor his mother had anything more to add and so silence fell upon the group. Just as the stillness began to become oppressive, Collin's voice dispersed the pall. "So, shall we partake of your mother's delightful breakfast?"

Liz smiled. "Yes, that's a wonderful idea!"

Jason turned toward the table and was surprised to see it shimmering half-heartedly in the summer sun. A quick glance at Collin told Jason he wasn't sure what was happening either. His frown revealed irritation more than confusion, but he quickly replaced it with a weak smile and added, "Maybe we should continue this another time, darling."

Jason frowned as his mother's cheerful voice rang out, "As you wish, Collin dear. That would be fine."

And before he could say another word, the picnic table ceased its shimmering and he and his mother found themselves back in their yard, dressed as they should be.

"Holy smokes!" came Scat's voice. "Did you see that?! Andy, tell me you saw that too!"

"Yes," Andy replied. "I saw that too, Scat. I very much saw that too."

Jason turned toward the two familiar voices and was never so glad to see two people in his entire life.

As much as she wanted to, Andy didn't ask Jason to repeat the story. Liz had disappeared to her room. Jason couldn't help but wonder exactly what was going on between his mother and Mr. Bastion, but for now he would honor her desire to be alone. Andy seemed to have some ideas on the subject, but none of them sounded promising.

"I'm not totally sure, of course," Andy began. "I mean how could anyone be? It seems to me that the ghost is trying to recapture his past. Your mother is the spitting image of the woman in the book. Although the book calls her identity 'unknown', the woman in the photo is linked to Collin Bastion. Further digging tells us that the woman had a child out of wedlock shortly before Mr. Bastion left the United States."

"You would think he would have known of her condition," Scat interjected, and Andy picked up his trail, continuing on without missing a step.

"Maybe not. The chronology gets a little shaky around that time. Her name appears alongside his in numerous newspaper clippings detailing social events that she apparently attended with him. She is referred to as his fiancée more often than not. There is no mention other than that, though, as to wedding plans or engagement parties. I would question whether the title of fiancée was just a social ruse."

"A social what?" Jason asked. He was floating in and out of the conversation, but this idea caught his attention.

"A social ruse," Andy repeated. "A scam of sorts. What the purpose of it would be I have no idea, but it makes the most sense."

Jason nodded, sliding out of the conversation again. Of course, a scam. Once a game player, always a game player; the question now became how to find out the current game.

Scat laughed. "Social events? This area hardly seems like a social mecca."

"It's not, and it wasn't. Mr. Bastion brought society with him and apparently took it away with him again when he left," Andy continued.

Jason listened with only half interest. Already the event was fading. It seemed so very long ago, breakfast. A glance at the clock told him it was only 11:30 AM; not so long ago after all. He stood and walked over to the window and looked out over the backyard, his eyes finding the picnic table. It was still set for breakfast and Spike made his way cautiously among the plates, glasses and silverware set for two. There was no food out there, so his interest was short-lived.

"No food," Jason said aloud.

Andy turned to Jason, repeating him questioningly, "no food?" She was not fond of being interrupted, but the present topic leant itself to differing opinions and she was running rapidly toward the end of what she had to offer. She was eager to share the floor with anyone who had something to offer besides jokes and side comments.

"There is no food on the table," yet there was food on the table when we were there. At the lake," Jason said.

"Meaning?" Andy's question was soft and inquiring.

"I'm not sure."

Scat and Andy exchanged glances. Andy finally spoke up. "Okay, let's explore it though. Can you tell us about the food?"

Jason continued to watch the table as he spoke.

"The setting was different too. These are from our kitchen. The plates and stuff at the lake weren't ours. I think the food wasn't ours either. I think that they never had breakfast, that he had only just gotten here and they went outside and then left from there.

That coming here was the only way to get there."

Andy frowned. Something didn't sound right. "I don't know Jason. How could he know?"

Jason turned toward Andy, eyes inquiring.

"How could he know that there would be a way to get to there from here?"

"Unless he can get there from anywhere," added Scat.

"Then why come here?" Jason finished.

The three sat in silence, each mulling one thought – what were they missing?

Liz sat on the edge of her bed, her eyes focused on the window, willing herself not to think about him. What had she done? She had never intended to involve her children in any of this. She had made that clear to Collin from the start; but he had pushed and so she had dangled the idea of meeting Jason in front of him like a carrot, and he had reached for it. She had only wanted to find out some things. He intrigued her, yet she seemed to be getting nowhere with her quest. Jason seemed to interest him, so she had done it. She had used her son as bait.

Liz buried her face in her hands, but no tears came. Deenie had not interested him, only Jason. Funny, she thought, lifting her face from her hands, I never asked why. Now it was too late. Liz frowned. No, this was still between Collin and herself. She was dabbling where she had no business. She had known it all along, but she had done it anyway. Okay, she said to herself, you did this; now you can undo it.

A soft knock on the door broke her thought. "Mom?" came

Jason's voice. "Are you okay?"

"I'm fi…"

Enough! She thought to herself.

"Come in, Jason."

He turned the doorknob and pushed open the door. His mother sat perched on the edge of the bed facing the window. She turned to greet him, her blonde hair framing her face like a halo as the sunlight behind it filtered through the strands.

"Let's talk," she continued.

An hour later Jason was still confused. Try as she might, Liz just couldn't find the right words, so she had done what she thought she would never do with her children. She lied.

CHAPTER 15

Jason's feet found their way out of town and before he knew it he was on the path and making his way through the rocks. Before long he found himself in the clearing. The spring gurgled its welcome and Jason couldn't help but smile. He sat on a small boulder and contemplated the pool, waiting.

"Some things are not meant to be understood through thought. Some things you must know with your heart."

The voice sounded like silk on the wind, and he turned to see who had followed him. No one was there. Jason turned back to the spring and, looking into its depths, was only half surprised to find a familiar face staring back at him.

"Hello, young one."

"Hello, Shanta," he whispered in return, bowing his head toward the pool.

Jason sat still and waited in silence.

He had first experienced Shanta when his parents were splitting up. It had been a rocky time for his mother and him and he had come here often. Shanta had come to him early one evening as the sun was going down. She basically told him to go home. The desert at night was no place for a man or a boy, and that night in particular was not a good one to be there. Jason had been startled, but not afraid, and heeded her warning.

The next morning he had awoken to find delicate frost crystals frozen on his window. The temperature had dropped during the night, unseasonably, and he would likely have frozen to death before he could have found his way out in the dark. He had been wearing only jeans and a short-sleeved shirt, not having considered going home until the time to leave was approaching. The air had remained warm even at that late hour of dusk, so he hadn't seen any concern in that regard. He was young, and foolish. And Shanta had saved his life.

They had spoken on occasion after that, and Jason had come to know that it was Shanta who determined when a meeting was necessary, not him. Over the years he had come here to find solace, sometimes in her words, but more often in the knowledge of her presence.

"Ask me what you must," came the silk on the wind.

Jason looked up, startled. She had never given him that option before. He whispered without hesitation, "Is my mother in danger, Shanta?"

Her reply came, as he knew it would, "Some things are not meant to be understood through thought. Some things you must know with your heart."

Sitting there beside the pool, Jason knew, with his heart, that his mother had lied to him. "She's in danger," he whispered.

"Your heart has wisdom," the wind whispered back.

Liz sat on the edge of the bed long after Jason had left. He had not questioned her meandering tale. He, as she, was stunned that she had spun it. He knows, he must, she thought to herself. How could he not know that was a lie? She sighed. She had never lied to Jason before, not like that, but she needed more time to sort things out. She needed to talk to Collin.

As though on command, she found herself rising from the bed and walking out of the room, down the stairs and toward the front door. She collected her keys and purse as she went and reached for the knob when the telephone began to ring. Once, twice, she waited for the machine to pick up.

"Mom? Jason? Anyone home?"

Liz raced for the phone. "Deenie! Angel, how are you? We've missed you so!" All thoughts were forgotten and she was herself again.

"Hey, mom. I've missed you too."

"How are things with your dad? Are you having a nice time?"

"Sure. I think Dad's sad now though. His friend doesn't like him anymore and doesn't come over like she used to."

"Dad's friend? Which friend is that, Sweetie?" Liz bit her lip. Anger welled in her. What did she care? Only because her daughter was there; other than that, she didn't.

"Jessica."

"I see. Well, I guess it's a good thing your dad has you for company then, right?"

"I don't know. He's not home much. I think he's trying to meet a new friend."

Liz's eyes narrowed. "If your dad's not home, Sweetie, who is taking care of you?"

"Miranda. She wants to say hi. Hold on."

The next voice on the line was that of a cheery elderly woman.

"Hello, dear, this is Miranda. Deenie has told me so much about you."

"Oh, well, that's nice of her. I'm sorry, but my ex-husband didn't tell me that my daughter, our daughter, was not going to be in his care during this trip." Damn, she thought, that sounded awful.

"Oh, that's quite all right," Miranda said, "No offense taken."

Liz frowned. She was sure that had been a silent self-admonishment. Miranda continued on, though, without giving it a second thought so Liz let it go as well.

"It is simple, really. Andrew, your ex, is a louse. I rescued your daughter, the mermaid princess, from the land people and gave her a magic potion so she could survive on land on her own until her mother, queen of the mermaids – I suspect that is you – could send her trusted dolphin steed – I believe its name is Jason? – to come and rescue her."

Liz could hear Deenie giggling in the background. Then there was some fumbling noises as Deenie tried to wrest the phone from Miranda, unsuccessfully, and Miranda continued.

"I'm sorry, I seem to have my fairy tales mixed up. The crux of the matter is that I have had the pleasure of your daughter's company daily for some time now and I thought it best that she call you and make you aware of what she is doing each day. You are her mother, are you not?"

"Yes, yes I am."

Silence. It was Liz's turn and she had no idea what to say. This was a nightmare, maybe, possibly, or not?

"Miranda?"

"Yes, dear," came the cheery voice.

"I don't know what to say. Has Andrew hired you to sit with Deenie?"

"No."

As an afterthought, Liz asked, "Does Andrew know Deenie is with you?"

There was some whispering and then, "I don't know."

"So I am to believe that Deenie just leaves her father's home each day without saying where she is going and comes to be with you?"

"I didn't say that."

Liz could feel her frustration rising. "Please put my daughter on the phone."

"Of course, dear. It has been lovely to meet you. I hope we can do this again sometime!" And she was gone.

"Hi mom."

"Deenie, what's going on honey?"

"Dad knows that I have a friend from the pool that I go spend my days with. He doesn't know it is Miranda I think; mostly because I don't think he likes Miranda and wouldn't let me spend my days with her if he knew."

"Why doesn't your father like Miranda, honey?"

Liz could feel her chest squeezing. Please God, she thought, please…

"Miranda helped me escape from the land people and dad got mad about that."

Liz didn't pretend she knew what that meant. She wished Jason were here with her. He would know.

"Deenie, do you want to come home?"

Deenie looked at Miranda. It saddened her, but she had no choice. "Yes, I do."

"Okay, sweetheart. I'll arrange it."

"Thanks, Mom."

"I love you, sweetheart."

"I love you too, Mom."

Deenie handed the phone to Miranda, who unceremoniously set it back in the cradle. "It's for the best, dear. This place is no place for a princess, that I know." Deenie smiled. Miranda was the best.

On her end, Liz slowly placed the phone back in the cradle, her eyes struggling to focus on something, anything, that would ground her back into her life. Damn him. Damn Andrew. Damn Collin. Damn them all. She could feel it rising inside herself; the familiar anger washing away the vulnerability and uncertainty. She picked up the phone and dialed Andrew. There was no answer, but she hadn't expected one. She put on a happy face and began her spiel. "Hello Andrew. This is Liz. Just calling to check in and see how things are going. I wanted to let you know that I am going to be heading out of town for a few weeks on Friday. I'm going to a mountain retreat with a couple of women friends. Originally I was going to take Deenie with me, but since she is with you, if you extended her stay to six weeks that would mean I could have the time to myself. Of course, it is at your discretion, but it would really help me out. Thanks, and let me know."

Liz set the phone down. No wonder the lie to Jason had come so easily. Two lies in one day. Where was she headed?

Andrew played back the message as soon as the light began to blink, signaling the caller had hung up. He had given up thinking Jessica would call. He missed her in an odd sort of way, but knew it would pass when the next Jessica was installed into his life. He listened to Liz's message twice, then deleted it. It was odd. Liz never lied, but that could hardly be the truth. It didn't matter anyway. The summer would improve if his daughter went home, so he'd put her on a plane on Friday.

The door opened as if on cue and in walked Deenie. "Hi Dad."

"Hey, bad news. Your mom called. She's taking you on a trip or something this summer and so I need to send you home."

"Ohhhh." Deenie feigned disappointment. "When do I have to leave?"

"Friday. I know you're disappointed, but that gives you a few more days with your friend from the pool. What's her name again?"

Deenie disappeared down the hall to her room and didn't say another word.

Jason walked slowly down the street. He was trying to figure out what to do next, but he had no idea. As he turned the corner to his street, it hit him. A chill passed through him as a sudden realization enveloped him. He saw no other way. He retraced his steps and headed to Andy's house. What he would tell her he wasn't sure, but it would be better than going home.

Great, Andy wasn't home. Now what. Her mother said she had headed to the library this morning and she hadn't seen her since. Jason had seen her since, but he had no idea where she could have gone. He had no jacket with him, which would be problematic when the sun went down, but he would have to make do.

This is silly, his subconscious told him. Go home and get a jacket. No! He seemed to scream back. I'm not going home until I get some answers! His insides raged like that until he found himself on Liz's front porch.

"Hello, young man," Ed said.

"Good afternoon, Ed. Marla," Jason replied, nodding to each.

"Liz is around the corner. She should be along any minute. Can I get you anything? Care to wait?"

"Sure, I'll sit awhile and wait." Jason rubbed his arms. "It sure is getting chilly."

Ed looked at Marla and shrugged. The temperature gage on the house read 82.

Not five minutes later, Liz came up the walk and Jason walked to meet her.

"Hey, I've missed you," he whispered.

Liz beamed.

"Supper's almost ready," called Ed. "Why don't you join us, Jason?"

Liz smiled, and Jason couldn't help but smile back. He hadn't eaten all day. It would be a long night and some food in his stomach would make sense.

Jason's edginess melted over roast chicken with apple and raison stuffing, green beans and gravy. By dessert he was laughing and the foursome rapidly lost track of the time. When the hall clock chimed ten o'clock, Jason came to with a start.

"Well, it's getting late. I should get going."

Ed and Marla smiled; they had decided it best not to concern themselves with the oddities of youth. Jason walked to the door with the three in tow and stopped at the threshold. He rubbed his arms again. Ed laughed.

"Here son, take it," he said, and reached into the closet for a light jacket for Jason. "That should do you 'til you get home."

"Thanks," said Jason, feeling guilty. He stared at his shoes, until Liz cleared her throat and he looked up to find them alone.

"You okay?" she asked.

"I've been better," he said, smiling weakly. "It's a long story, and one I want to tell you. Tonight I don't have time, though. I have to be somewhere."

"Be somewhere?" Liz queried.

"Oh, well, yes, be ho…"

He couldn't do it. He couldn't lie to her. He took her arm and pulled her out onto the porch and quietly shut the door behind them.

"I'm sorry. I can't tell you right now. I'm not going home. There's something I have to do tonight. I can't tell you what because without the whole story it wouldn't make any sense. I can't lie to you either though, so that's the most truth I can share right now."

Liz had no idea what he was talking about, but she knew whatever it was it must be important. She smiled, "it's okay. We'll talk about it tomorrow then."

Jason brightened. "Great! Tomorrow." He hoped with all his heart that the tomorrow in her mind would happen.

Jason left the walk with a final wave and headed toward his house, or at least made it seem that way. No point in messing up this early in the night. He could hear the phone ringing in the house behind him. Someone must have picked up the receiver, as it ceased mid-ring. Who would be calling Ed and Marla at this hour? He glanced over his shoulder one last time and lengthened his stride.

"Liz, honey. Telephone."

"Thanks, Uncle Ed."

Liz took the phone from him. "Hello?"

"Liz, it's Andy."

"Hi, Andy. Are you okay?"

"Yeah, sure. Is Jason there?"

"Jason? No, he just left."

Andy was silent, so Liz added, "He said he was headed home."

"He said?"

"No."

"No?"

"Right."

Andy frowned, then it hit her. "Thanks, Liz. That's a huge help. I'll see if I can't head him off."

"Goodnight, Andy," Liz said and hung up the phone.

Uncle Ed appeared in the doorway. "Kind of late to be calling around. I hope everything is okay."

"Yes," Liz smiled. "Well, goodnight Uncle Ed," and peeking her head into the kitchen, "Aunt Marla. Thanks for having Jason over for dinner. It was a lot of fun."

"Yes, dear, it was," said Marla. "He's such a nice young man."

Ed watched the exchange, and then shook his head and moved into the kitchen to fetch Marla. "That's enough work for one day, Marla. What's left will keep until tomorrow."

Liz poked her head back into the kitchen, "I'll finish up in here. You relax."

Marla laughed and let Ed wrap his arm around her and steer her towards the front porch. She pulled away at the last moment, but he held her tight. "I have your sweater right here, so don't you go making excuses." Marla laughed again. Once on the porch, Marla wrapped the sweater around her shoulders and then let Ed wrap her in his arms as they settled into the porch swing.

"Those kids…" Ed began.

"Hush now, Ed," Marla cut him off. "This is our time, the kids can wait."

Ed looked at her and laughed, then leaned his head in towards hers and breathed in the sweet night air laced with the fragrance of her hair.

Jason kept up his pace. He wanted to put as much distance as he could between himself and Liz's house in case someone decided to come looking for him. When he reached the corner of his street, he headed off in the opposite direction. He glanced once over his shoulder, not really expecting to see anyone, and lengthened his stride for a second time. Time was passing and he had somewhere to be.

Andy reached the corner out of breath and barely had time to duck into the shadows when she saw Jason turn away from his street at the corner and head off in the opposite direction. There could only be one place he was headed. "Damn it," she muttered. He glanced back once, but not expecting to see anyone, he didn't notice her standing at the tree line. Andy took a deep breath, held onto the stitch in her side and took off after him. This was not what she wanted to be doing tonight, but there was no way she was going to let Jason go back to the lake alone.

Jason made good time and reached the lake before midnight. He made his way to the overlook and then continued on down the path that he had followed Andy down. The night of the school dance seemed like eons ago, but it was more recent than he cared to think about. And now he was here again. He felt a breeze kick up and pulled Ed's jacket closer around himself and zipped it. He made his way through the reeds and entered the long grass that surrounded the lake. How different it had seemed at breakfast. So neat, like a park. Jason shook his head. "Stay focused," he muttered to himself.

"Oomph."

Jason froze, barely daring to breathe. Someone else was here. He turned slowly, crouching low, and headed off to his left. He would circle back and come up behind whoever had followed him.

"Not so fast," came a familiar voice, and Andy appeared in front of him.

"What are you doing here? Jason hissed.

"I'm happy to see you too," Andy replied, "and I think I could ask you the same question." She folded her arms across her chest, cocked one hip and waited.

"Okay," Jason said, "but tonight is not the time for this. You need to leave."

"So do you."

"I will, but there's something I need to do first."

"I'll wait," she said, unmoving.

"No, you can't. I need to do this alone."

"Jason, whatever you plan on doing, it will only make it worse."

Jason was preparing a comeback when he stopped short. "What did you say?"

"I said whatever you are planning will only make it worse. Jason, listen to me," Andy continued, putting her hand gently on his arm. "I know what you're trying to do, but you can't fix it this way. Your mom has to fix it, not you."

"My mom?" Jason was confused.

"What's going on has nothing to do with you and these horses," Andy continued. "It's bigger than this, deeper than this." She waved her arm to the expanse of the lake and the fields. "This is like, say, cranberry sauce at Thanksgiving dinner. Whether it was prepared or not, the meal would still go on. If you hadn't ever come here that night, your mom's situation would still be going on."

Jason knitted his brow. He was confused. "My mom's situation?"

"Yes, this is her situation. This is her situation with Collin Bastion."

The name jolted Jason back to his senses. "What are you saying, Andy?"

"I'm saying your mom opened the door and let Mr. Bastion in. She is the one who will have to show him out again through it."

Jason looked at Andy hard. "Let him in?"

Andy could see this was going to be harder than she thought, so her first priority was to get Jason out of here. Time was growing short. She could feel the mist begin to climb up her legs as it made its way from the reeds to the shore of the lake. It wouldn't be long before they weren't able to find their way. The time to act was now.

"Where's your mom tonight, Jason?" Andy asked.

"Home."

"Alone?"

Jason's eyes flashed, telling Andy all she needed to know.

"Maybe we should go check on her. It's getting late. Midnight's a bad time to be alone, don't you think?"

Jason smiled. "Okay, Andy, you win. We're going."

They turned together and headed back toward the path. Jason could hear the sound of snorts and snuffles in the distance, a sign that the herd was growing restless. They left the reeds and headed up the path that would take them out of the lake valley, only when they reached the overlook, Jason took Andy's arm and pulled her toward it. Andy hesitated, and then gave in. They were out of the path of the horses, which was what mattered. This would only take a moment.

They sat down side by side and watched the misty figures in the distance. "You hear that?" Jason whispered.

"The horses?" Andy replied.

"It's more than that, more than just the horses. It's the sound of…"

"Two worlds colliding."

Andy and Jason both jumped, scrambling back from the edge as fast as they could. Laughter surrounded them, ricocheting off the rocks around them and then tumbling into oblivion over the valley.

Andy moved to make a break for it, but Jason grabbed her arm and held her fast. If Collin Bastion was here, that meant he wasn't with his mother. So far, so good.

"Mr. Bastion!" Jason called out.

"There is no need to shout," came the reply, eerily close. Jason fought the urge to recoil from the breeze of the breath. Andy had her eyes closed and stood rock still. Jason eased her into a niche between a boulder and the rock face and let her go. She released his arm and seemed to melt into the rock.

"Why are you here, boy?" The question was pointed, one for which no answer but the truth would do.

"I came to speak with you," Jason replied.

"Then speak," came the reply, and Jason found himself face to face with the essence of Collin Bastion.

The essence of Collin Bastion was far different from the form Jason had seen that afternoon. The being was smaller, barely five-feet tall, and had sparse gray hair that wisped around his head like a sparsely iced cake. He had some sort of waistcoat and britches on; what exactly its color was hard to make out, as he tended to fade in and out. When he spoke, he became brighter. When silent, he faded.

"Well, boy?" A hint of impatience peppered his speech. "What is it?"

"You look quite different," Jason began, trying to keep the frown from his face.

"I hardly think that is what you came here to discuss," Mr. Bastion replied.

"No, it's not."

"Well, good. At least we are in agreement on that."

Jason's frown deepened. Something was off here. Very off. He took a step closer, which Mr. Bastion matched with a backward motion. Jason gave a quick glance in Andy's direction and continued his awkward advance.

"Why are you doing that, boy?" Bastion's irritation was evident this time, and Jason took another step before replying.

"You know, something tells me you are not exactly who you say you are." He hoped he was right. Jason wasn't sure what happens when you call a ghost a liar.

Much to his surprise, the result was instantaneous. The small being disappeared and was replaced by a larger form.

"No, he is not me." Jason backpedaled. Before him stood the real Collin Bastion, of this he was certain.

"That was Preston. He is my valet and as such is predisposed to attend my needs as I see fit."

There was nothing more being offered, so Jason tried to fill in the gaps. "How many of you are there?"

Collin eyed him curiously. "Only one. How many of *you* are there?"

Jason realized how silly the question was and racked his brain for another. Collin had no desire to wait, ending their conversation before it had chance to begin.

"It is late. You are to take your young friend home and proceed to your own home thereafter. Do you understand me?" Jason was somewhat taken aback, but decided that discretion was the best course of action and nodded curtly.

"Good."

Jason eased himself back to where Andy still clung to the boulder and whispered to her, "Hey, Andy, we're going home now." He unwrapped her arms from the boulder and took it in stride when she wrapped them firmly around his waist. He put his arm around her shoulder and guided her back to the trail and up the path toward the road.

Collin Bastion watched them go. When they were out of sight he shook his head slightly. So close, yet he could not risk it with the girl present. She knew too much as it was. He had played it well and neither of them suspected. That was what mattered most right now.

Preston appeared at his side, but Collin dismissed him with a wave of his hand. Not tonight, old friend. Not tonight. Tonight there was much to think about.

Preston faded off, wondering if he should follow the boy or simply wait until he was summoned again. The wave of a hand was a vague command at best. A good valet interpreted vagueness of that sort as a desire for discreetness, not a dismissal. What had his father always told him? Don't wait for a command; act on the need for a result. Preston glanced back at his master. Collin had his back to him. He was lost in thought, as usual. Preston moved quickly, gliding up the path. They couldn't have gotten far.

Once they reached the road, Jason breathed a little easier. He had hoped Andy would to, but her eyes remained firmly shut and she continued to rely on Jason to help her find her way. Once out of earshot of the lake, Jason began a whispered conversation with her, hoping to get her attention and maybe a response of some sort.

"Now that wasn't so bad, was it?" he began.

Nothing.

"I think we learned a lot tonight. Or at least…"

"Shhhhh!" hissed Andy.

Jason was startled, but went with it. He held his tongue for a moment and then whispered, "What is it?"

"He can hear you."

Jason glanced around him. "Who can hear me?"

"Him."

"Andy, I really don't think…"

"Shhhhh!"

And with that Andy stopped. She refused to budge, and Jason, anchored to her side by her arms, stood with her. She was frowning in concentration, then opened her eyes, turned to her right and pointed her chin at the trees and whispered, "There. He's there."

"Who's there?"

"Him."

Jason sighed. "All right then," and without a second thought, Jason called out, "Hey you, in the trees, come out."

Before Andy had a chance to cringe, Preston wafted before them as quick as a flash, an annoyed fire in his eyes.

"What do you want?!" the little man croaked, obviously miffed at being found out.

"Nothing, I…"

"Good!" screeched the being, cutting him off mid-sentence, and it vanished.

Andy relaxed a little at his side, and began to walk again. They walked in silence until they reached Andy's house. He waited at the end of the walk until he saw the light in her room go on and then headed for his own house. The day had started out strangely and seemed to have grown progressively worse.

As he neared his house he saw the lights glowing. That wasn't a good sign either. Jason let himself in through the front door and found his mother asleep on the couch. He pulled a throw blanket over her, clicked out the light and headed up to bed. Hopefully tomorrow some of this would make more sense.

When she heard Jason's door close, Liz opened her eyes and pulled the blanket tight under her chin. It was three o'clock in the morning. Where had he been all day? And all night?! Tomorrow. Tomorrow they would sort all of this out. They had to. Deenie would be home in a few days.

CHAPTER 16

Jason awoke, remarkably at ease. Sunlight played across his cheek with the promise of a beautiful day. He smiled despite himself, and stretched languidly under the covers. He wrapped himself around his pillow and watched a bird as it flitted among the tree branches outside his window. He would have plenty of time to think about the events of the last week, and especially last night. For right now, this was all he wanted to do. He just wanted to watch the bird.

Without warning, the bird grew agitated and flew away. Jason sighed as Spike sauntered into view, balancing effortlessly on the branch. Spike was equally at ease walking in the treetops as he was on the ground. Years of practice had made it so. The bird had made a wise decision to give up its tree and move on. Jason felt a prickling sensation at the back of his neck. Years of practice… comfortable in two places… comfortable in two worlds! Jason sat bolt upright, kicked off his covers and rummaged for a pair of cutoff sweat shorts and a t-shirt. He bolted down the stairs, calling "Mom!" as he went.

Liz hadn't slept much last night, so the cool sunshine and the promise of a glorious day was a welcome addition to her morning. She had two choices, and she wrestled with both. Does she do this alone and dismiss the entire thing with no explanation as a mother's prerogative, or does she confide in her eldest child, her son, who probably knows some of what she would share with him anyway?

Liz suspected Jason knew more than she thought, so dismissing it entirely without explanation would set a precedent in their relationship that she wasn't sure she could bear. She had always treated her children with honesty and respect, hoping that her influence in the years she had them alone to herself could undo the years of broken promises and puffery that their father had vested them with. Jason had thrived under her influence, just as he had railed against his father's chicanery. He had an innate sense within him that guided him in a loftier way.

That sense had also been a source of inspiration and guidance for her over the years. There had been many times that she had unconsciously followed Jason's lead on decisions regarding her daughter and her ex-husband. She had told herself that it was because the children should have their own choice in matters regarding their lives, but when she was honest with herself she realized it was because Jason had a deeper sense of what was spiritually best for them all. He had no hidden agenda, as she and Andrew often had. He saw things clearly.

She frowned slightly, wondering if this gift was one of childhood and if maturity would taint it in some way. She reflected on his anger at Deenie's visit to her father's. Was that a sign of maturity? A crack in the gift perhaps? She laughed to herself. No, he had been dead-on with that one as well. This trip was most definitely not the most spiritually rewarding for her daughter. Her laughter faded though as thoughts of her daughter rekindled memories of her conversation with the strange woman, Miranda, who was her daughter's daily companion. She mumbled, "I'm sure she's harmless," to herself as the sound of Jason's door burst open and the word, "Mom" reached her. She took a deep breath. Here we go, she said to herself, and turned to greet her son as he made his entrance.

"Mom!"

"Yes, Jason, I'm here."

Jason bounded into the kitchen, yet when mother and son finally were face to face, both became sheepish. Both had been eager for the other's company, yet now the odd tension that had tugged at them all week seemed to spark as Jason came through the door. Liz moved forward and took her son in her arms, hugging him tightly as though the act could smother the spark and end the tension. Jason balked at first, but the familiarity melted him and he hugged her back hard, harder. Again harder, until both began to laugh and broke apart only because their laughter-weakened knees would no longer support them.

"That felt good…" Liz began, wiping a tear of laughter from her eye. Jason watched her, and when Liz glanced his way she could sense a familiarity of sorts really had returned. "Laughter is good for the soul," she continued. "It helps."

"I get it," Jason laughed, and Liz laughed along with him.

Liz straightened and looked her son in the eye. Time to clear the air, she thought. As she watched him smile, she balked. No, not quite yet. She wanted to enjoy his company like this for just a while more before she told him the truth.

Jason was famished and struggled to eat the three scrambled eggs, bacon and toast his mother made for him at a reasonable pace. He tried to remember the last time he had eaten and the memory of the dinner with Liz and Ed and Marla popped into his mind. Crowded right behind it was the memory of the lake, and Andy.

Andy! He needed to call her, to see how she was.

Jason and his mother had chatted casually while his she cooked, neither delving into anything complicated or threatening. Jason had steered clear of any mention of the horses in the front yard and Liz gave the time traveling breakfast adventure at the lake an even wider berth. When they had exhausted the triviality halfway through the browning of the bacon, Liz brought up Deenie. She had told him he was right, letting Deenie go with her dad at her age was probably a mistake. She then recounted the strange conversation with the old woman, Miranda. Jason laughed, and Liz felt better.

"Do tell if you can make heads or tails of that gibberish," Liz requested.

"It's a game Deenie and I used to play when we went to the pool. She can't swim so she won't leave the steps. She made up a game where she's the mermaid princess trapped on the steps by the land people and she waits there for her dolphin steed – that would be me – to rescue her."

Liz listened intently, Miranda a forgotten issue over the reminder of the closeness of her son and daughter.

"I swim laps and when I'm done I come and 'rescue' her from the stairs and ride her around the pool a while. We haven't played that game in a long while, though. I'm surprised she even remembers it."

"Your sister remembers everything," Liz interjected. *Everything*, she emphasized silently to herself.

"That was great, Mom," Jason said suddenly, hoping he

wasn't ending breakfast too abruptly.

"You're welcome. Well, we both have things to get to, I'm sure," Liz continued. Jason was up in an instant, brought his dishes to the sink and turned on the water.

"I'll get that…" Liz added. Jason turned with a grin, kissed her cheek, and added, "You are the best!" Liz watched him go and thought to herself, then why don't I feel that way?

Jason slipped the phone off the cradle, glanced back at his mom, and then thought better of it. A conversation here, now, would not be the best way to handle this. He took the stairs two at a time, peeled out of his clothes and jumped in the shower. Ten minutes later, hair still wet, he was headed out the front door. He had called out that he was leaving, backtracked to the kitchen to kiss her cheek, and then slipped out the back door instead of the front before she had a chance to ask him where he was going. Jason was out the driveway before she had a chance to wonder, or so he thought.

In the kitchen, Liz bit her lip. Whatever he was up to would come out later, just as what she was up to would. She walked slowly to the front window and lifted the curtain slightly. She could just make out Jason's form as he turned the corner from their street and headed off. Bless this countryside, she thought. On a clear day you really can see into forever. She returned to the kitchen to give it a once over. Everything was in its place. She was free to go.

Standing in front of her bedroom mirror, Liz looked closely at her face. She looked tired. She lifted the lid of her jewelry box and pulled out a locket and chain. She caressed the cover, and then released the hasp to reveal the two old black-and-white photos inside. The woman was on the right and wore a high-necked, cream-colored gown; her hair swept up, piled almost on top of her head. She was smiling, almost with a Mona Lisa-esque effect. She knew something, maybe some secret she shared with the photographer.

The man's photo, in contrast, was straightforward. His hair was dark and short; a jacket, shirt and cravat formalized an otherwise jovial expression. He had mirth in his smile and in his eyes, so much so that when Liz had come across the locket at a rummage sale she had purchased it, eager to learn more about its occupants. It wasn't until she had shown it to Miss Carl at the library that she noticed, or rather Miss Carl had pointed out, how much Liz resembled the woman in the photo. When Liz had asked who she was, Miss Carl brought out the old archive book and showed her the picture of Collin Bastion and the accompanying photo of the unknown woman.

It was odd, she thought later on, that Miss Carl had not asked her where she had gotten the locket or had inquired about obtaining it as an artifact for the library. This concern seemed to bury itself, though, as she delved deeper and deeper into the life and history of Collin Bastion. It was barely three weeks later, after having read every reference she could find relating to him, that she had written the note in her best, most elegant penmanship and slipped the note into the pages of the archival book.

She didn't know why she did it. It was a crazy thing, really, to write a note to a person who no longer lived here; likely no longer even existed. If he did still exist, he'd be well over one-hundred years old. Yet she had written it nonetheless, and here she was staring at the photos again, wishing she were that woman and knew the source of that secret smile.

Liz closed the locket and heard it gently click shut. She undid the clasp on the chain and placed the chain around her neck. This would be the last time, she told herself. It had to be. She stood and went down the stairs and through the kitchen to the back door.

She looked out into the yard and, drawing a deep breath, opened the door to step outside.

Almost immediately she found herself stepping out onto the large veranda of a country home. The porch was as wide as it was deep and disappeared around the corners of the house to the right and left. An ornate, white railing ran before her and disappeared around each corner as well. Directly in front of her, the railing gave way to wide steps that floated gracefully down to a rich, green lawn. The air was thick and sweet with the smell of freshly mown hay, perfumed with wisteria. As she glanced around, she noticed scores of other blooms whose scents were begging to be noticed, but who were no match for the force of the dominant one. It's funny how life repeats itself, she thought, over and over again, all around us.

Liz made her way to the top of the stairs and was surprised to find Collin not far off. He was astride a large, black horse and both stood still, staring at her, like one statue. The horse's nostrils flared slightly, giving away the life that pulsed beneath the still exterior. Collin watched her for another moment and then nudged the horse forward. They covered the ground to the base of the steps at a leisurely pace; the sudden sound of crunching gravel marking their progress up the pathway. An equally abrupt silence marked their arrival.

"I was not expecting you," he commented.

"I was not expecting to come."

Collin looked away. Now was not much different than it had been then. Life had a way of repeating itself, over and over, even in death. It must end though, eventually, he thought.

"Shall we walk? Perhaps talk?" Collin asked.

"That would be nice."

Collin extended a hand and nudged the large animal

sideways.

Liz walked down a few steps, brushed his fingertips with her own, and continued down until she stood beside the two, seemingly undaunted. Collin sighed and dismounted. Pulling the reins over the horse's head, he offered Liz his arm and the threesome walked silently up the walk.

Silence followed them for a while. Liz was content to take in the scenery. She had never seen such lushness before; at least not in this part of the country. I wonder, she mused silently, am I still in 'this part of the country?' She had never concerned herself with the details before, but today she wondered. Maybe today would be different indeed.

"Yes, you are," came the audible reply.

Liz was not surprised. He had a habit of that. She would have been more surprised if he had not commented. He held his tongue on the latter part of her musing though. His first thought was to answer no, but maybe today could indeed be different.

"Can I tell you a story, Lizette?" he began.

"Of course."

"When I was a young man, I met and fell in love with a woman."

"Lizette?" queried Liz.

"Yes, Lizette," he continued, unfazed.

"I came to America, to this part of America, to find pastures for my horses. England was becoming too small for me and so I wanted to find a place where I could be free." He hesitated, drew a deep breath, and then continued. "I wanted to be free of the obligations that my future held and the propriety that those obligations demanded of my youth. My solution, as I saw it, was America. I would bring the family's herd to America where they would thrive on the lush pastures to be found here. They, and I, could roam free."

Liz listened intently. Her face was masked with a gentle smile, yet her heart raced beneath her moderate exterior, so much so that she could not imagine him seeing through it; seeing through her…

"For a while, this was indeed the case," he continued. I found and acquired the property around the lake. The rock walls that surround it provide a natural barrier for the animals, sparing them the confines of fencing. They could roam their valley as they pleased, never once considering themselves constrained, and I could take solace in the knowledge that they were indeed contained."

He grew more animated as he talked about the horses. He always does, Liz thought to herself. This story was about more than the horses, though, of that she was sure. She strengthened her resolve and her composure and tilted her face towards his, cocking her head to better hear him, even though his words were loud and clear.

He glanced at her, reading her face and continuing his story with an answer to what he believed to be her unspoken question.

"As for my home, we are now on the far side of the lake. The trees separate us from the lake and the valley. It gives the horses their privacy. I purposely built the barn among the trees. It offers shade and acts as a buffer between us…"

He looked at her again, and sighed. "But you don't really care about that. You didn't then, and you don't now."

Liz knew better than to speak. If she wanted the story, she

needed to hold her tongue, and so she did.

"Where was I… ah, yes, I constructed this oasis for us all and brought the horses here. Forty head in all - one prime stallion, which you see here," he indicated toward the large black horse that followed him like a large dog on a lead, "and several lesser stallions. I had no desire to mix with American stock, although I didn't dismiss the concept entirely. I just wanted to be sure I didn't have to. So, forty head of horses, thirty-five mares, five stallions." He drew a breath as though to begin again, but did not. His chin dropped slightly, something Liz had never seen happen, but it regained its perch before an untrained eye would have caught it.

"Being in a small town, it was quite impossible to keep entirely to myself here. So I soon found myself the center of the social scene. History varies on this account," he said with a quick laugh, "as to whether I brought society with me or society took advantage of my arrival and sprung up around me. Which doesn't really matter, but it happened, and before long there were balls and tea parties, and comings-out to attend. And so I did. It was Preston, my dear friend and valet, who warned me of the dangers of attention in such areas, as his sharp ears were already picking up fabricated affections between myself and several of the eligible young ladies in town. Were they true?" He glanced at Liz, looking for a reaction, and seeing none, continued on. "Some, maybe, inadvertently; but believe me, once news of their public knowledge reached my ears I was quick to redeem my morals and apologize for any forwarding of friendship that propriety did not bear in this society, which was so different from my own at home. People understood, or more likely they did not want to slap the hand that provided them such life and vigor, and so apologies were accepted, boundaries were established, and I found myself back under English reign, frustrated and at wits end."

"Go on," Liz whispered. "I am enthralled."

Collin turned sharply to look at her, and could see she truly was, and so continued, despite having had no thought to the contrary.

"Then, Lizette arrived." With this, Collin stopped, deep in thought. He turned to face her, his eyes searching hers, "I must tell you now, before we go further, that under normal circumstances I would never have allowed it to happen. I would never have…"

Liz's eyes met Collin's and for a moment she could feel it, the deep sadness that held him. Just as suddenly it was gone. He turned away and resumed walking. As he continued on with his story, his tone seemed to have acquired a composed edge. The window into his heart had snapped shut.

"Lizette was the ward of a friend of mine in England. The letter I received from him conveyed that she was wild and free, that he could not contain her and so he was afraid for her in England. Honor is such a tenuous thing, and a woman's honor so easily besmirched in England… I readily agreed to have her here to see if the wide-open spaces of America couldn't set her right.

"Lizette arrived one week later. It seems she had been put on the next boat after my friend's letter, him knowing me well enough to know I would never deny him.

"Well, the talk in the town was not to be believed. Scandal? Not really, only that I had sent to England for a bride, and this was my betrothed. At first I was shocked. She was, after all, barely a woman; but later I realized that this small lie could serve many a purpose. It would keep the ladies from me, and the gents from her. In short, it would, and it did, allow both of us to travel freely in society with one another, allowing each to enjoy its offerings without having to fend off its curses. I conferred with Lizette, who, in hindsight, agreed much too readily to the arrangement. It wasn't until it was too late that I learned of the mischief she already had at work. I will not frighten you with the complexities of our ruse, but will only confer that in time the lines began to blur quite badly. So badly, that I soon found myself in love and betrothed, but with no marriage pending." And at this, Collin turned to Liz, looked her directly in the eye, and stated crisply, "Ever."

"Oh dear," Liz exclaimed.

"Yes," Collin said. "Oh dear, indeed. Lizette had taken full advantage of me, and in the end I mean *full* advantage." He looked at Liz, who blushed for him despite herself.

Collin composed himself and continued the narrative.

"Lizette and I were constant companions. We dined together - breakfast, lunch and dinner. She learned to ride so that even then I would not be without her. Any and every social event included her, as quickly as the 'Men Only' events ceased to occur. We had no cause to be apart, and so we were not. We were happy, or so we seemed. Since I can at this time only speak for myself, I will say, 'I was happy.' I really don't think I could ever have been happier. Lizette was my equal in every way. Our downfall, then, lay in the areas where she attempted to lay claim to an equality that she had no stake to. A man must be a Lord of his manor, and that Lordship cannot be shared, not totally; not even with his Lady. To that end, I made one rule. She was not to go to the valley. My horses were not to be disturbed.

"I should have known better, but youth has no wisdom in such matters. Lizette read between the lines and decided that there was a place she had no admittance to. It became her mission, therefore, to gain admittance to this sacred territory of my heart.

"Lest I confuse you, or take this tale to a length that incites boredom, I will hurry the conclusion. Lizette could not gain admittance to the valley in my heart where the horses dwell. I had oft hinted at marriage to her, but she avoided the subject deftly and I did not push. I would wait, as was my manner when it came to her, until chance presented the appropriate opportunity, or she brought the idea to me. When our indiscretions finally resulted in her being with child, I believed the opportunity to have arrived and pushed the issue of marriage with her again. She refused. Her price for changing her mind was admittance to the Valley. She would rather live besmirched with the mark of a bastard child than be Lady to a man who kept parts of his heart from her.

"Youth does strange things. I loved her, more than life, yet I would not be abused and bent like a piece of soft tin. I refused, and she left. Just like that, one day, she was just gone. I waited, quietly, for word of her arrival in England and the scandal that would follow, but she had much worse in mind. She simply disappeared, the scandal now being mine alone. The rumor that her leaving was prompted by her being with child had already begun, and now she was gone. A town knows what it wants to know, though, and the rumors swirled and settled into nothing. Their loyalty was to me, or rather to my attentions."

He stopped. Liz knew there was more, but still he stopped. "I am not Lizette," Liz stated simply.

"I know you are not," Collin replied. "You wanted to be her, I wanted you to be her, but we cannot make it so."

"I'm sorry," Liz said, which sounded silly after the saying.

"I know you are," he said.

They were quiet for a while. As they walked along, Liz finally asked, "Why the library?"

Collin smiled. "All my things are there."

Liz laughed, and he laughed with her.

"I will miss you," she said.

"You don't have to," he said.

"Yes, I do. My daughter comes home tomorrow."

"Ah, yes. And what of our son?"

"Jason?" Liz grew wary.

"What will you tell him?"

"The truth."

"Good. He needs to know."

After a moment, Collin continued.

"After you left, the horses began to die. Did you kill them?"

Liz remained silent. She didn't have the answer and suspected there was no right one. Collin continued on without one. "I had to ask. There was no explanation; only death. One by one, by one. Death."

Their walk had taken them full circle. Collin indicated the steps, and Liz put her foot on the bottom one.

"It was never the same, was it?"

"No, it wasn't."

Liz rose another step, then turned, a worried look on her face. "Collin?" she asked, the rest she dared not say aloud.

Collin passed the reins over the horse's head and mounted easily. "No, you are not Lizette; cannot be Lizette," he answered. "The boy, though, will be our son."

Liz's blood went cold. Before she could reply, he spun the horse and cantered away. She sat down on the step and put her head in her hands. She had to collect herself, somehow. Her family needed her. When she lifted her head moments later she found herself seated on the steps to her own back porch staring at a pair of sneakers.

"Mom?" Jason asked, "are you okay?"

* * *

Jason had made record time and arrived at Andy's house puffing hard. She was on the front porch, swinging lazily. She had two glasses of lemonade with her and handed one to Jason after he plopped down next to her. He took a sip and waited.

"Some night last night," Andy stated.

"Sure was," Jason replied.

"Here's the deal," Andy said, continuing to look straight ahead, "things aren't exactly what they seem. Collin Bastion isn't interested in your mother. He's interested in *you*."

"Me?" Jason replied, startled. "What makes you think that?"

"He's looking for his son, Jason."

CHAPTER 17

Jason reached down and took his mother's hand, pulling her to her feet and wrapping her in his arms. He buried his face in her curls.

"Jason," Liz began, "I'm so sorry…"

"Shh," he cut her off. "Not yet, Mom, not yet."

They held one another for another moment and then walked together into the house. Liz sat at the kitchen table and Jason poured them each a glass of water. Liz played with the water as it beaded on the outside of the glass; Jason watched her fingers play along the glass.

"You were going to tell me something," Jason began.

Liz looked up. Where to begin. She looked into his face and smiled. He really did look remarkably like Collin, a much younger Collin. Then, she asked, "Jason, can I tell you a story…"

An hour later, Jason sat digesting the tale Collin had shared with his mother. She unclasped the locket from around her neck and laid it on the table. Jason picked it up and turned it over in his hand. The back was engraved; it had one word on it written in an ornate engraver's script. "Jason."

"Where did you get this?" Jason asked.

"A rummage sale," Liz replied. The conversation seemed so usual, so normal.

"So it's true?" Jason whispered.

"I don't know what 'true' is anymore," Liz confided. "If you mean, does he believe you to be his lost son, then I suspect that is 'true'."

Liz was surprised at the conflicting emotions welling inside of her. The protective ones she could understand. She was a mother, after all, and that was her forte. It was the others, the sense of anger at her loss, the desire to be able to fulfill her dream, to consummate her fantasy, that surprised her. Hadn't she had enough? Why was she still clinging to this cheap, dime store romance she had created? Wasn't the rest of her life meaningful enough? She frowned, and the words came out unbidden. "I had hoped to end this. I went to him to end this."

"You went to him again?" Jason started. Liz cringed at his words and tried to salvage her logic.

"It's all right. It is over."

Then the tears welled up and she couldn't stop them. It wasn't over. If it wasn't over for Jason, it wasn't over for her.

Jason's eyes flashed red. "It ends now," he said. He rose from the chair, scooping up the locket as he went. He needed answers, and he knew where to get them.

A short time later Jason found himself on the path to the nappe. He made short work of the journey through the rocks and within minutes was on the plateau. The gurgling of the spring greeted him, but today it only angered him. He took his usual seat on the rock at the edge of the spring, waited a moment, and then glared into its depths.

"I know you're in there," he snarled. He didn't really expect a response, but he needed to vent.

"You lied!" he seethed under his breath.

"Tsk, tsk, tsk," came the reply, soft and silky.

Jason was stunned, but his surprise only served as a temporary cap for his anger. It continued to roil beneath the surface, waiting for a chance to escape again. Jason glanced at the water again, and waited. Nothing. Irritated, he picked up a stone and began to finger it. An idea struck him. Casually, he tossed the stone straight up and caught it, tossed it up and caught it, tossed it up and caught it, right over the pool. After a dozen or so such exercises, he allowed the stone to drop. It splashed into the water and tumbled to the bottom of the shallow pool in a swirl of bubbles. Jason smiled and reached for another stone. He repeated the exercise – toss and catch, toss and catch, toss and catch – only this time he allowed the stone to drop after six rounds. It hit the water with a loud "thunk" and spiraled to a rest not far from the first one.

Jason looked into the pool and noticed for the first time that its floor was entirely of sand. Odd, he thought, to have a sand pocket in the rock, but not unheard of given the water. It won't be a pocket for long, he thought with an angry smirk. He reached for another stone and continued his game. This time, dropping the stone after four rounds. He immediately reached for another and allowed it to drop after two short rounds. He reached for yet another rock when he noticed that the bubbles from the falling stone had not subsided. Instead, they were growing more violent. The small pool was rapidly becoming a bubbling, churning pot of water. He considered stepping back, but decided against it. He would see this out. He did, after all, start it.

Tossing up another stone, he waited to hear it strike the water and when it did not, he looked into the pool to see a seething reflection of himself staring back at him. The reflection held the stone at the water's surface for a moment and then hurled it back at him, hitting Jason squarely in the forehead.

Jason tumbled backwards off the rock. "Damn it!" he cried, unbidden. He regrouped enough to ask," What did you do that for?" When no response came, he added, "Shanta?"

"Hardly," came the saucy, masculine reply; the silken voice forgotten.

Jason proceeded cautiously. "Okay, then who?"

Laughter. Loud and harsh, almost a shriek, boiled the water in the pool. When it was able to regain control of itself, the being replied, "I am Jason."

Jason's eyes narrowed, "How do I know you aren't lying again?"

"You don't," the being said, short and clipped.

"Great," he muttered.

"Oh, don't be so maudlin," the being continued, its voice suddenly relaxed and casual. "You really aren't being much fun today."

"Fun? Today? How long have you known me?"

"For as long as you have come here. You're not very bright today either."

Jason ignored the last comment; he was fixated on a growing sense of embarrassment that he had been duped, conned, hoodwinked – all this time – into believing he had been confiding in a woman spirit, but all along it had been this crass boy.

"So that's what I've been all this time? Fun for you?" Jason could feel his anger resurfacing.

"Well, of course. What else would you be?"

Jason hesitated. Was it really that simple? He took a deep breath and shelved his anger. He had come here to get answers, so that was what he'd strive for. He began again, on a different tack. "If you are Jason, where is Lizette?"

"She is gone."

That was simple. So far so good, thought Jason. He pushed on, gently.

"Gone where?"

"I don't know. She will tell me when she returns."

"Ah, so she comes and goes?"

"Of course."

"Is she Shanta?"

Shrieking laughter again. "Of course not. She would be furious if she knew I was speaking to you."

"Why is that?"

"Because I am dead and you are not."

Both Jason's thought those words would shock him, but they did not. He took some comfort in them. Maybe it was the surety of the statement, the nonchalant ambivalence of it; for whatever reason it sat well.

"Does that bother you?" The question could have come from either, but the being had asked it, and Jason answered confidently, "No." He let a moment pass, then added, "Are you stuck in that pool?"

"It is my home."

"It seems sort of small."

"It was larger until recently."

"Point well taken. Shall I restore it to its original size?"

The being hesitated, and then said simply, "No."

Jason waited a moment, and then quietly asked, "What will happen to me if I touch the water?"

Without hesitation, the being replied, "I will steal your body. I will make it my new home."

Jason nodded. "Thanks for warning me."

Silence again. Long and deep. Jason crept forward a little to get a look into the pool. It was clear and looked cool. Out of the depths, the voice washed over him as clear and cool as he imagined the water was. "I don't want to hurt you. Do you want to hurt me?"

"No," Jason answered. He waited a moment and then added, "I'd like to help you."

"Do I need help?" the being answered, intrigued.

Jason pondered this thought, and then decided to be straightforward. "Maybe it is I that needs help."

"Yes," the being said, "Yes, I believe it is you that needs help." And then after a moment, it added, "Maybe we both need help?"

Jason smiled. "Yes, maybe we both need help."

"Maybe we can help each other," the being stated.

Jason felt a moment of doubt, but brushed it off. Maybe they could help each other.

"Jason," he asked, "can I tell you a story?" and with the being's permission he told him everything he knew.

It was near dark when Jason drew near the house. He had been careful on the trip home from the nappe to avoid Andy and Anna's house. Right now was not a good time to get trapped in long conversations. He approached the house and opted for the back door. It would seem more usual, or so he hoped. He stopped outside the door with his hand poised on the knob and whispered to himself, "Well, here we go."

"Yes, here we go," came the soft reply.

Liz had already made dinner and was keeping it warm for him. She hugged him hard when he came in, like a long lost soul come home. He felt a shift inside, and pulled back from her. "Dinner ready? I'm famished," he lied. Food was the farthest thing from his mind.

Liz chattered easily while they ate. The strain of the week was still evident in her face, but she ignored it and kept to safe territory. Out of mind, out of sight, Jason thought, and smiled to himself. Deep inside, he could feel the beginnings of a giggle and he coughed to mask it when it tickled the back of his throat.

"That was great," Jason said, pushing his plate away. He had barely touched his meal, but Liz made no comment on it. She collected the dishes and moved to the sink to wash them. Once her back was to him, Jason spoke to it.

"I ran into Andy on the way home. She wanted to..."

"That's fine, dear," Liz cut him off. "Don't be home too late."

Jason sighed, grateful. It was better this way. No looming lies.

"Thanks, Mom." He rose to leave, then came up behind her and whispered, "I love you" as he kissed her cheek. He moved to the back door.

"Jason," she called, never once turning her face in his direction. "Be careful in the dark."

He hesitated only a moment, but she heard it and understood. "I will," he answered.

As the door clicked shut, Liz whispered, "I love you, too" to the still house, hoping it would help, somehow.

Once outside, Jason headed once again for the lake. It was the most logical place, had always been, to find what he was looking for. And after what his mother had shared, he had another plan of attack. Jason had always heard there was a road that wound back behind the lake. Why no one had ever explored it he had no idea. It just never held anyone's interest for long, much the way other things concerning Collin Bastion didn't hold people's interest for long. This held his interest, though, and he intended to see where it led.

Jason passed the cutoff to the overlook and continued down the road. No one really came this way, not even in their cars. He wasn't sure the road actually led anywhere. It was another of those mysteries that might solve itself when he learned to drive.

Then he could explore these uncharted paths better. For now, though, his feet were his locomotion and he had never had the need to pass the lake. Tonight was different.

The rocks gave way to long grass, as far as the eye could see. Maybe the road was overgrown. Great, he thought to himself. His eyes scanned the grass, looking for something, anything. There! He walked on a bit farther and strained to see through the thick grass. It looked like a pole of some sort. Maybe the post to a gate? He started to head into the grass, but jerked to a stop. "What the hell?"

His feet seemed to take on a life of their own as he found himself retracing his steps back to the overlook. He scrambled down the path, hugging the edge of the rocks and then the edge of the pasture. Barely five hundred yards from the rocks was a small path that headed into the woods. His feet took it. Another hundred yards later the path dumped onto a crude road. A quick look around showed him the gate he had seen was now between him and the main road.

The road was overgrown, but identifiable and very passable. Jason whispered, "Thanks" into the air and felt a nonchalant "Your welcome," come back at him. He smiled. They were on their way.

They made good time and it wasn't long before the wooded borders began to give way to what once could have been a more manicured, landscaped environment. Jason stopped and pulled the locket out of his pocket. He carefully undid the clasp and put the locket around his neck. He took a deep breath and whispered, "Ready?" He nodded to himself in affirmation, and closed his hand around the locket. He began to walk again, this time more slowly, his eyes and mind trained on another time.

He wasn't sure what to expect, but he did expect something to happen. When nothing did, he couldn't help but feel disappointed. There he stood, in the fading light in the middle of literally nowhere. Now what? He turned and looked back the way he and his counterpart had come. The road was beginning to disappear in the shadows. It wouldn't be long before it would be impossible to find. He sighed and asked himself, "Any ideas?"

"Press on," came the silent reply, and so he did. Grasping the locket again, he turned back to continue his trek when the area ahead came alive with light. Jason moved off the road and ducked behind a tree. He wanted to present himself on his own terms so it would be best to stay out of sight until he was ready. His feet told him the ground beneath his feet was no longer choked with weeds, and he looked down to find a velvet carpet of lush green that not even the fading light could dampen. He smiled. Inside, a voice said, "It seems we are here."

The sound of hooves on gravel made Jason shrink even farther into the shadows. Voices drifted toward him, the words still too far off to hear, but the sound of laughter peppering the banter evident. Jason stood still and waited. The riders, two of them, soon drew abreast of him. It was a man and a woman, both finely appointed. The man led a third horse, which lacked only a rider, by a lead.

The man rode an enormous black horse that melted into the night with the all-but-faded light, giving the illusion that the rider simply floated on air next to his companion. The woman rode a slightly smaller gray horse that tossed its head now and again as if it were in on whatever humor was tickling its rider. The woman, in turn, gave no notice, her attention fixed on the protocol of interaction with her companion. When they reached Jason's tree, the man reined in, looked directly at Jason, and asked, "Are you going to join us, son?"

Jason was frozen. Inside, he could feel the laughter begin to bubble again and his body moved of its own accord from the shadows. It was no use, he was not the pilot anymore.

"We have been looking all over for you," the woman said,

mirth still evident in her voice. Whatever the search entailed, it was not a stressful one, he surmised, as his body approached the horse. I can't ride! he thought, a moment of panic hitting him, but his autopilot reassured him, taking the reins from the gentleman, passing them over the neck of a rather feisty looking gray colt, and swinging effortlessly into the saddle. The colt sidled sideways playfully, to the evident mirth of the gentleman and lady alike, but soon settled down as the threesome moved on with their journey.

Jason could feel the rhythmic movement of the horse beneath him and found a part of himself musing, "So this is what it feels like to ride a horse." He was reassured to go with the flow by his companion, so he settled in for the ride, despite the foreignness of this new side of himself.

Once they were underway, the woman split her attention between the man and Jason. The light from the driveway lanterns lit her face and Jason was surprised at the comfort he felt in his new role. The woman, Jason knew, was Lizette. Part of him saw her as his mother, although he had never seen her in this form before. Part of him, a fading part, saw her as only resembling his mother. The man was unknown to him, although he knew him to be Collin. The oddity of the arrangement of his knowledge pricked at him, and he knew it did so with good reason, but his present situation left him with few options. So he tried to neither struggle against it nor lose ground to it with moderate success.

The horses made short time of the walk to the house. Collin alighted gracefully and then turned to assist Lizette. Jason dismounted with equal grace as three grooms materialized out of the shadows and moved off into the night with the three horses. Lizette took Jason's arm and directed him towards the house, all smiles and affection. But one look into her eyes foretold of a deeper smoldering that her forced levity could not hide, and Jason could feel all of him shrink from her reflexively. Collin's smile froze on his lips. Jason noticed it and Lizette's eyes found it as well, fanning the flames once before she was able to contain them again.

"Lizette," Collin began, his eyes on Jason, "we will dine in the long hall this evening, so a change of clothing is in order."

Her eyes flashed again. "Of course. I will show Jason to his room then..." She reached for Jason's arm, but Jason sidled away and Collin filled the breach. "No, he and I have a few things to discuss before we find our way to dinner." Collin turned his eyes to Lizette, "I'm sure you understand, darling. Man to man?" The question hung there, poised and pregnant. Jason realized what was happening, and was relieved when Lizzette merely bowed her head and left the room with a rustling of her riding habit. The crop she carried struck her boot with a loud sting as she passed through the doors and out of sight.

Collin watched the empty space of the door she passed through for a moment and then turned to Jason. "Well, we have quite the predicament now, don't we?" His face hardened as he continued, "What the hell do you think you are doing?"

Jason struggled for control of his words, but his body was not his own anymore, and that included his tongue. "Dad?" came the voice, higher than Jason's and belying a younger soul.

Collin's eyebrows shot up. He searched Jason's face, then whispered, "How..."

"Did I do good, Dad?" came the youthful voice again, pleading.

After a long pause, the answer came. "This cannot be."

Jason could feel the roiling start long before Collin could, but the eruption, when it came, was fast and furious. Jason could feel himself hurtling through the air, arms reaching to grab hold of something. Nothing. He crashed into the ground in a heap at Collin's feet. The roiling stopped instantly on impact and Jason sat up, rubbing bruised knees and elbows. Collin's face clouded over and he reached down, lifted Jason roughly by the arm and held him firmly. With his other hand he grabbed a handful of hair and held his head still while he looked intently into Jason's eyes. He searched and appeared satisfied, but something caught his eye, and his scrutiny intensified. "Ah, there you are," he said, smiling. He released Jason, allowing him to slump slowly back to the floor. Collin walked several paces, slowly, then spun on his heels and asked, "Does your mother know?" The youthful voice answered sulkily, "No." Collin laughed. "There, my young friend, I am afraid you are mistaken," he said. "And what about yours?" he directed to the still slumped form. When no response was forthcoming, he frowned. "Youth. Impetuous youth," he muttered to himself. Then, glancing at his pocket watch, he turned and strode from the room, calling casually over his shoulder as he went, "Dinner is in half an hour. Proper attire will be expected," and he was gone.

Jason felt his control return, and with it, anger. "What was that all about?" he seethed at himself. "We'd better do as he says," was the only reply. Jason stood, shakily at first, but regained his composure when Preston entered the room. Startled, the valet let slip an "Oh," that expressed more than he had cared to. He peered at Jason, then peered a little closer, then drew back as if suddenly discovering the object of his attention was a rattlesnake. "Oh," he said again, this time with no effort to mask its meaning.

Jason stood where he was. "Your move, old man," he thought to himself. "Your father has asked that I show you to your quarters, sir," came the explanation for his presence. "Very well," bubbled from Jason's throat before he had time to formulate a thought, and Preston turned and marched off with Jason, fast on his heels.

Once washed and dressed, Jason perused himself in the fulllength dressing glass in his quarters. He hadn't noticed, but suspected, that the clothes he wore were not his own anymore.

They weren't. He frowned at this. This wasn't really going as he had expected it would, but then again, what had he expected? He began to wonder if he was already in over his head. He could feel the beginnings of a giggle that did not bode well either.

He turned from the glass and began to walk toward the door. Rather than fight it though, he decided to wait. Go along for the ride, he thought, for now.

CHAPTER 18

Jason entered the dining hall to find Lizette seated alone at the table. She sat completely still, poised, with an inviting smile on her face, almost like an animatron waiting for its cue to come to life. Jason walked to the seat opposite her and contemplated her features. Her blue eyes were cloudy; it was as if she wasn't there, but rather was off on some important errand and had hung a 'Be right back' notice in her eyes. From within he heard, "She's traveling."

Collin entered abruptly with a clicking of heels on the rich wood flooring. Lizette blinked once and came to life in a rush of activity. Exactly like an animatron, Jason thought to himself. Collin moved to Lizette's side of the table and kissed her cheek before returning to his own seat at the head. He sat and Jason followed suit. Almost immediately, a flurry of kitchen staff entered and filled the wine glasses and soup bowls, then were gone. The entire exercise took barely two minutes. Collin grabbed a loaf of bread and tore off a large hunk, from which he in turn tore a smaller ragged piece and then dunked it vigorously into his soup. He placed it thoughtfully into his mouth as he perused his two companions.

"Not hungry?" he inquired of both. Lizette glanced at him with a smile. "Soup is not my favorite, darling. I will wait for something more to my taste."

"Ah," he replied, turning his attention to Jason.

Not knowing what to do, Jason reached for the bread. Lizette gasped and her hand flew to her mouth as if to stop the flow of sound. Collin was one step ahead of her and grasped Jason's hand before it could retreat with the bread. With his other hand he removed the bread from Jason's hand and released him. He set the bread just out of reach, and leaned back in his chair, his fingers forming a steeple to support his chin. Jason, still shaken up from his obvious error, sat up ramrod straight. His back was molded to the back of the chair, creating a wide buffer between himself and the table with its apparently forbidden contents. He had no idea what had just transpired. Neither of them did.

"It seems," he began, his gaze flickering between Lizette and Jason, "that we are four for dinner." He waited for a reaction. Lizette dropped her eyes; Jason met Collin's gaze, unaware of what he should be abashed by.

"Good," Collin said, meeting Jason's gaze. He turned back to Lizette. "You have lied to me, darling." Lizette cringed, but even in that she stood tall. "You lied to OUR son." The words cracked like a whip, and turning back to Jason, he continued, "and now in turn our son has lied to this boy."

Jason could sense his insides recoiling in fear, but not his own.

Lizette raised her chin at this accusation. An odd response, Jason thought, but it caught Collin's eye and it was indeed her response. He watched her closely.

Despite their pleasantries and smiles, Collin and Lizette carried on their true conversations in a language all their own. The flicker of an eyelash, the twitch of a cheek, the flexing of fingers;

their words continued on, sounding like just what they were: idle comments for the benefit of whoever cared to hear them. The actual heat of their words was exchanged in silence.

Lizette communicated mostly with her eyes and the carriage of her body; Collin with his hands and face. Lizette's eyes smoldered when angry, belying an ancient well of acrid fire that had never, and possibly would never, die. Collin's anger was not so deep, yet. It was a surface wound that, if left unattended, would likely fester and spread to prove a formidable match for the smolder of his companion. For now, though, it did not have a life of its own, it merely flared in response to her heat.

Their silent raging continued, until Jason could stand it no longer. He cleared his throat loudly and said, "Excuse me." The two stopped, mid-glare and mid-twitch, and turned to stare at him, surprised and somewhat bemused.

"Please, why may I not eat anything? I'm really rather hungry."

Jason was not sure whether it was he or the being that had expressed the sentiment, but it was a desire shared by both, and as such both eagerly awaited the reply.

Collin looked at him, looked at Lizette, and began to laugh. It started as a low rumble, deep in his gut, but soon it came forth in booming waves. Lizette watched his laughter, then looked at Jason, who was also beginning to giggle. She soon found herself trying to hide her own giggles, ineffectively behind her hand.

The four laughed together for a good long while, after which Collin turned to Lizette and, abandoning his signals, asked her in words, "Why, darling, do we carry on so, when we are capable of such joy, as a family?"

Lizette's laughter faded and she was pointed and sharp.

"You know why."

"I don't." Jason heard the youthful voice come again from his mouth and held his breath.

Lizette looked his way and hissed at him, "You are in enough trouble."

"But why?" the voice asked again. Then, as pointed as his mother had been, he asked her, "Why don't you want me in your family?"

Lizette was aghast. She looked like she had been slapped, hard across the face, and her response to the offense was silent shock. She had no answer. The truth was in her actions, not in anything she could say, and she knew it. For as long as she could remember she had spent her time here, with Collin, in this partial family, in an arrangement that did in fact exclude their son. Never mind she had created this arrangement to hurt Collin and Collin alone. How long ago was it now, his unforgivable offense? And had she, had they, really never made their peace over it?

Lizette frowned, dropping her eyes, trying to find the answers. Answers she knew she didn't have.

Jason could feel himself rising, and the small voice inside asked him, "Please take me home, back to the pool. It seems it is where I belong."

Jason looked wildly from Collin to Lizette and back to Collin. That was it? Just like that? They couldn't possibly let this be the end.

"No," said Collin firmly. "You are welcome here, son. You are always welcome here." He turned to Lizette, and waited. She did not respond.

Collin felt one hundred years old suddenly. "This bickering, this angst, it is pointless," he continued, "and I won't do it any longer." He looked pointedly at Lizette, then his eyes softened, and he continued. "You have my heart, foolish woman. You always have. I may have pretended to have a stronghold of will, but whatever stronghold I ever possessed turned to dust the day you arrived at my door. My love for you is greater than your spite for me could ever be. Why else would I have allowed your games all these years? Your silly comings and goings, Preston has known your destinations and the whereabouts of our son for centuries."

Lizette looked at her hands throughout his speech, and then coyly looked up with a melting smile. He continued. "I do these things for you, my love, always for you. It seems, though, our games are not our own anymore…"

"We have been silly, haven't we…" she said.

A giggle slipped past her lips, and soon they both were lost to it. The laughter grew and soon brought tears to their eyes. Collin slipped from his seat and went to her side. Grasping her hand, he pulled her from her seat and spun her around the room in large, lazy, endless waltzing circles; both Jason's forgotten.

Jason stood with his jaw open in amazement. "What just happened?" whispered the being inside him.

Jason hesitated a moment, and then answered him. "Love just happened."

"What is love?"

"Love is… well… a feeling that is not containable."

"Oh."

Jason wondered, and then asked, "Don't you feel love?"

"For who?"

"Well, for your mom, or your dad, maybe?"

"Why should I?"

Good point, Jason thought, but he pressed on. "Love is a feeling that isn't really explainable. It is one where you just feel strongly about someone and so you feel protective and don't want any harm to come to him or her. You think of them first, usually, before even yourself. And you'd feel really, really sad if you knew you wouldn't see them again."

"Like you feel about your mom and Deenie, and about Liz," the voice said.

Jason thought about it a moment, and then simply said, "Yes." Then he added, "And how I feel about you."

Jason felt the being inside him growing before he had finished saying the words, like he was outgrowing his clothes, only he was the clothes. He groaned a little and beads of sweat popped on his forehead. The growing continued, unabated. "You have to get out," Jason croaked. "You're... crushing... me." He barely got the words out before he felt the room go dark. He could hear the sound of feet as he hit the ground and their vibration on the cool, stone floor as he lay there. There was shouting, but he couldn't make out the words. They were too far away and his ears were too full. All of him was too full...

Jason awoke to darkness. He was frightened for a moment, but then realized the sounds and smells were all familiar. He was home, in his bed. He sat up, got his bearings straight and went to the door. He cracked it a moment and listened. He could hear voices, several of them, coming from the kitchen. He crept to the top of the stairs and listened.

"I'm sure you understand, this was not any of our intention.

Boys, as you know, will be boys. Neither of us had any inkling that our Jason was in contact with your Jason. If we had known, we would have stopped it immediately."

A soft, feminine voice cut in, much softer than Jason had recalled from his experience of it. "You have a remarkable son, Liz. His heart knows no bounds. I think he has taught our Jason some valuable lessons."

Collin continued, "He has taught all of us some valuable lessons."

Jason could imagine his mother's face, and it made him smile. He almost fell to the floor, though, when he heard what followed.

"A game," Liz repeated, angrily. "So this whole thing, from start to end, has been a game?" She looked first at Collin, then at Lizette, his companion.

Lizette raised her chin a notch and Collin squeezed her arm, begging patience.

"You must understand," he began, only to be cut off by Liz's terse demand. "*Must* I?" she insisted, her tone firm and clear. Keep your head, she thought, yet images of the past weeks swirled through her head. She knew if she went there she would be forever mired in it, whatever it was, so she forced herself to remain in the present, in command.

"You are correct," Lizette said, slowly and firmly, "You do not have to understand. Yet, you do have your role in all this, do you not?" She waited, eyebrows raised, expectantly.

Liz sighed. Yes she did. And she looked at the woman, really looked at her, for the first time. Oddly enough, they looked nothing alike. A game, Liz said, it is indeed a game.

"This is what you do?" Liz asked, "Play games?"

Lizette smiled, the air suddenly light. "Yes," she replied, perhaps somewhat too gaily. "Do you not play games to amuse yourself?"

Not like that, thought Liz.

Collin began again, hoping to bring the interview to a close. "So we are all in accord then, that no harm was intended and no harm was done?"

Liz wanted this over, needed it to be over, so she asked the only logical question left. "And what happens now?"

Lizette and Collin looked at one another, at a loss.

Liz whispered, "You don't know, do you?"

"No," Collin whispered back, "we do not."

Jason heard Liz coming his way and he scrambled silently back to his room. Liz climbed the stairs, opened his door and came to rest at the edge of his bed.

"I know you're awake. I also know you were listening at the top of the stairs."

Jason opened his eyes and looked at his mother in the murky light. She looked the same. Did he?

"Do I look the same?" he asked.

She laughed, "Yes, of course you do."

Liz leaned forward and kissed his forehead.

"Do we want to talk about this?" Jason asked.

"I don't know," Liz answered. "If it will help you, yes. If it won't, then it's over. You know more now than most people do, about what, though, I don't know. Maybe it is just for you to know and it is best if no one else does." She watched her son, hoping.

Jason thought hard for a moment. He understood what she was saying, and agreed inside, for the moment at least. "If I need to talk about it someday, can we?" he asked.

"Of course!" Liz exclaimed.

Liz ruffled his hair and got up to leave. I wonder how much longer I'll be able to get away with that, she thought. Such a simple thing, ruffling my son's hair, so packed with meaning, yet one day…

When Liz got to the door, Jason called out to her, "Mom, will I ever see them again?"

Liz looked back at him and for a moment she felt afraid. There was only one real answer, so she gave it.

"That's up to you, Jason."

She turned and left, closing the door softly behind her.

CHAPTER 19

Friday seemed like a brand new day. Jason rose early, downed a glass of juice and left in a flurry of sneaker laces and wet hair.

"Where are you going?" his mom called after him. "Deenie will be home at 4 PM!"

"I'll be home before that," he called back, and jogged the whole way to Liz's house. When he got there, Ed and Marla were already up. They had a hearty breakfast of buttermilk pancakes and bacon on the table with pure maple syrup fixings. Jason slid into the chair next to Liz and reached his hand under the table. He squeezed her hand. This was what love was all about, he thought to himself; when someone else comes first.

"You really didn't have to go to so much trouble over some berries," Marla chided him, but Jason wouldn't hear anything of it. He and Liz had promised Marla berries form the picking farm and that was the first order of business for the day.

Jason packed in four pancakes and three slices of bacon before he pushed back to initiate their departure. Marla had pulled two berry buckets from the shed and they were clean and ready to go. Liz kissed her aunt and uncle good-bye and took Jason's hand as soon as they were clear of the front gate.

"You look like your week improved since I saw you last," she began, smiling inquisitively.

"Quite a bit," Jason said, and pulled her hand to his lips and kissed it.

True to his word, Jason was home early. They collected Deenie at the airport and at 7 PM Ed, Marla and Liz came over with fresh baked pie. The two families sat down together, marveling at how they could live so close for so long but never sit down for coffee. Deenie vied for the center of attention, but the banter among the women-folk was too much for her. She snuggled in between Jason and Liz and allowed the reverie to play out like a picture show and lull her to sleep. Jason lifted her gently, tucked her in around 8:30 PM and caught the phone on the second ring on his way back downstairs. It was Andy.

"You sound great," she said. "Everything work out okay?" Her tone was hesitant.

"Everything worked out great," Jason said, and Andy found his enthusiasm to be somewhat unnerving.

"Great," she said. "We'll talk about it at a better time?"

"Actually, no."

Andy was floored. She didn't know what to say.

"When you're ready then," she said, trying to keep the dialogue open.

"There's really nothing much to talk about, Andy," Jason replied. There was no bitterness, no shortness; nothing but cheer and good tidings, but Andy heard a finality she had never witnessed with Jason before, and it spooked her. "It was all a game; a hoax if you will. Chalk it up to experience." Not quite a lie, he thought, but close. Semantics, actually; Andy could appreciate that.

They said their good-nights and Jason returned to his family.

Liz gave him an inquisitive smile when he returned and Jason replied, "Andy says 'Hi,' everyone." The reverie continued with barely a pause.

After she hung up the phone, Andy stood watching it for several minutes. She didn't expect him to call back. She didn't expect to call him back. She didn't know what she expected, but it hadn't been what she had just gotten. Not from Jason, anyway. She went out to the porch and sat down on the swing. She looked out over their short yard and across the street, her eyes flitting over the trees. It was a nervous habit, even though it spooked her. "Looking for shadows in the shadows is a dangerous way to begin the night" her mom used to tell her. Her eyes flitted a while longer until they saw it. A shadow. And it was moving fast. It scooted up the street, hung in the trees for a while, and then scooted on. She couldn't make out what it was, just that it was black. Black on black, only every now and then she could swear she saw a glint of moonlight off of something metallic.

When it was gone, Andy went back into the house. She locked the door and headed for her room. Breathe, she told herself, just breathe. It was bound to happen, she told herself, it had just been a matter of time. If you look for shadows in the shadows long enough, sooner or later you will find one.

Andy picked up the phone and called Scat. Normally she would call Jason for these types of thing, but things had changed, had shifted. Scat answered on the first ring.

"Hi, Scat," she said, not realizing how obvious the quaver in her voice was.

"Andy? You alright?"

"I just wanted to hear a live voice," Andy said. She held her breath, waiting for an answer. This was the point in the conversation where Scat would start building walls, making sure she kept her distance, kept it light. She waited, cautiously.

"Well, you've come to the right place," Scat said. "I'm guaranteed live and alive."

Andy didn't spook easy, but something definitely had her bothered. Normally this would be the time when Scat begged off, but something had turned in him. He had spent too long as a friend on the edge. It was time to get into the fray. He pressed on. "Light or heavy, your call," he said.

Andy smiled despite herself. Yes, things had definitely shifted.

Jason listened dreamily to the conversation winding down, and at 10:00 PM showed Ed, Marla and Liz out the door with a promise to return the clean pie plate the next day (Jason's mother would not hear of Marla going home with a dirty pie plate). As Jason watched them recede down the street, he noticed a shadow pass by them and shoot around the back of the house. He quietly closed the front door and followed it. As he rounded the corner, he felt something pass through him, almost like walking into a spider web. It didn't give way quite as it should have. Whatever business the shadow had was short, as it was already on its way out.

"Preston?" Jason whispered into the night.

Instantly the valet appeared before him. "Yes?" he said, in a tired voice.

"I'm sorry, Preston. I didn't mean to disturb you, but what are you doing here?" Jason looked around, and then his eye caught the glint of moonlight on metal. He walked over to the bird feeder, and he could hear Preston's voice in the breeze saying, "Master Jason wished for you to have it." Jason pulled the locket from the hook. When he turned, Preston was gone, as he knew he would be.

Once in his room, Jason sprung the catch to look once more at the pictures of Collin and Lizette. To his surprise, the faces there were no longer theirs, but his own and Liz's. He ran his finger over the back of the locket to trace the word, 'Jason' with the whorl of his index finger. It felt odd, so he flipped the locket and looked at the engraving. The word 'Jason' was gone, replaced with the word 'Marcus' in the same ornate engraver's script. He smiled and closed his eyes and tried to imagine the last few weeks, but they came to him only in a blur of bits and pieces. He turned his attention, instead, to the spring. The spring was now just that, a spring; no more, no less. For him, though, it would always be more, as would the valley.

He turned his thoughts to the horses and the valley. Some things, had not and would not, change. He looked at the calendar on his wall and smiled. Tomorrow was a full moon. The horses would be running.

The End.

ABOUT THE AUTHOR

J M Steele grew up in the magical and wondrous state of Connecticut. She now resides in Central Florida with her husband, Ken, their cat, Jill, and a head full of stories begging to be written.

Made in the USA
Columbia, SC
10 October 2024